The Goddess of
Lust, Love and Infatuation

Written By

Champagne

P.O. Box 841

Tobyhanna, PA 18466

(973) 348-5067

sspublishingcompany@gmail.com

www.sharsheypublishingcompany.com

Copyright © 2017 Sharon Terry
ISBN: 13:978-0-9972668-8-7
ISBN: 10:0-9972668-8-0
Publisher: Shar- Shey Publishing Company LLC
Book Cover Designed by: Dynasty's Visionary Designs
Edited by: ATW Editing

Table of Contents

ACKNOWLEDGMENTS

Thank you my Lord and Savior for giving me the strength and ability to complete this book.

I would like to express my gratitude to the many people who saw me through this book.

A special thanks to my parents Shirley and Eddie and my children, Khendaijah, Damon, Kristal, Dammond, John, Sharron, Jaquan and Jermaisha, for support and patience. Shameka, Sandy, Kimberly and Lamar, for encouraging me to live my dream.

Thanks to Shar-Shey Publishing, Editors and Designers for the crisp editing and stunning book design—without you this book would have never found its way to the web or printed books.

CHAPTER ONE

~ The Genesis ~

Growing up, Heavenly was an extremely happy little girl. She had both parents in the home. Every day she would see her parents embrace each other and also show her and her siblings lots of love and affection. As a young girl, she was very confident and loved to smile. Her only wish was to one day grow up and have love like her parents displayed. The love filled their home every day as they would have dinner. Their parents were so interested to hear what happened to them daily, so everyone would be anxious to tell their story. This was part of their daily routine Monday through Friday. Saturday they would spend family time on a variety of things such as cleaning, shopping, board games and other fun activities. Sundays would always be given to their church and getting ready for the next week.

Many things started to change drastically for Heavenly and her perfect world of comfort. She started noticing her dad was there more alone because her mom was working long hours. As time passed on, her dad confronted her mom about being gone so much from home. They began to argue every night and Heavenly would place a pillow over her head to block out the noise. Her parents would be so loud, sometimes a pillow could not help block out her parents' voices. She could not sleep, so she began to peek through the heater vents to make sure they were not hurting each other. Heavenly would always wonder how they just stopped arguing and then there was total silence. "Maybe one of them is dead and the other is covering it up," she thought to herself.

She started listening more to her parents argue and realized her mom was causing the issue. She would hear her mother stroke her father's ego by verbally seducing him with kind words. As usual, her father would accept these words of seduction as a form of honor to control his angry emotions. He was no longer angry because his heart was filled with kinder thoughts as her mother had successfully made love to his mind. Her mother thought she had calmed his spirit, but he still deceitfully yearned for freedom. He seemed at ease, but he was seeking to keep peace between the two of them and fulfill his selfish needs. Both Julian and Christine thought they were masters of the situation, but they forgot two things—their children and each other. Julian sought comfort from a longtime family friend, as Christine began to smother herself in fun at local bars. They both continued this behavior until it finally drew them apart. Julian moved out and Christine moved on.

Heavenly and her siblings were left to take care of themselves during evening hours. She was not aware of what happened, but she knew things had changed. The love she had for her siblings would not allow her to tell them what was going on. Instead she started using all the skills she was taught. Heavenly could run the whole household by herself, but her parents were too busy to recognize she was already doing that. She had great influence on her siblings and was already looked upon as their second mother. Being helpful to her parents had paid off. Whenever they would mention their parents, Heavenly gave her siblings an excuse because she didn't even know the answer to their questions.

Heavenly would often stay up late just to see when her parents came in and what their behavior was like when they came home. Often, one by one, they would come in and go straight to their bedroom, never noticing Heavenly sitting there. Their behavior was strange to Heavenly because she had never been ignored or walked past by both of her parents. Her mom would walk past her some of the time without acknowledging her, but her dad never showed this behavior.

*****

Heavenly begins to think something is going on with her parents, but she does not know what is happening. She begins to write everything she sees and hears in a journal her dad bought her. Her parents are looked upon as perfect, loving parents who are successful and happy. She knows if she speaks with any adults in her family, they will not accept her suspicions without proof.

She walks up to their bedroom door to listen for any arguing or yelling, and she hears sounds of someone crying. As she puts her ear closer to the door, she realizes it is her mother and she wants to know why she is crying. She goes to her room and opens the heater vent as she has often done in the past. While trying to spy on her parents, she realizes the other side of the heater vent is closed, so she can only hear what is happening in her parents' room. Heavenly closes the vent and goes back to her parents' door. Now it sounds like her dad is crying. Heavenly wants to know what is going on, but she can't see anything, so she is relieved to hear both of them crying and not yelling as they normally would do.

4

As she lies across her bed, she gets an idea to help her find out what happened with her parents that night. "I will go to my parents' room and ask Mom what she will be cooking for dinner. Maybe then she will confide in me as she always does. If she cooks, we can have dinner as a family like we used to do every night," she thinks as she smirks, turns over, and goes to sleep.

When Heavenly awakens, she is very excited to go through with her plans to put her family back together. She wakes up her siblings for school as she is getting ready herself. She gets dressed and follows through with her routine. She has to fix breakfast for her siblings every morning. As she is searching through the cabinets, she discovers that the food is very low and she only finds a few packs of oatmeal.

There is something awfully wrong and Heavenly has to find out what is going on because her parents had never let the food get low enough to see straight through the cabinets. She is devastated about her findings and tries to conceal her feelings of disappointment so her siblings are not alarmed. She gathers her thoughts, serves them breakfast, and gets them ready for their bus.

As she is sitting at the table, awaiting her siblings' bus, she gets into her thoughts: "Mom or Dad have not awakened from the noise we are making. They must have had a rough night." She needs to talk to her parents about their behavior which is affecting the whole family, mainly her siblings who cannot understand how serious this has become.

Heavenly puts her siblings on the bus and proceeds to walk back to the house. As she is walking slowly to the door, she thinks twice about questioning her parents. After all, she was taught better than that. She knows if she approaches her parents in the wrong manner she will be punished for questioning an adult, but she is willing to risk being punished to get to the bottom of this.

She slowly walks up to the door to listen, but there is complete silence. She knocks first as she has always done, but her knocks are unanswered. She knocks again, waiting for one of her parents to answer the door, but there is still no answer.

Sometimes her dad leaves early for work, and her mom may be in the bathroom. Heavenly debates about entering the room unannounced, but she decides to enter anyways. As she enters the room, it looks as if both her parents are sound asleep, so she begins to walk toward the bed. As she takes footsteps to reach the bed, she is totally shocked by what she sees. She is stuck in a long, blank stare as her heart races and she becomes weak. As she takes her last step to get as close to the bed as she can, she becomes more nervous as she reaches her mother's side of the bed.

There lies her beautiful mother, nude and sound asleep. Her eyes glance to the other side of the bed and there is a strange man, nude, and definitely not her father. Heavenly immediately dies on the inside from the devastating sight before her. "Is my mother a prostitute or an escort?" Heavenly thinks to herself.

She kisses her mom on the forehead and slowly walks out of the room. She turns to look at her mom and the nude man in the bed before exiting. She has mixed feelings of anger and confusion. She feels lost. All of a sudden, she instantly gets angry. She loves her father dearly and she doesn't think he knows about this man. Something bad has happened to her dad, and she is going to find out what has happened.

Heavenly is not thinking straight, but she wants answers. She doesn't care how she has to get them. She looks around the house, feeling confused about how she will get answers from her mother about what happened to her father.

"Did this man do something to my father and take my mom as a hostage? She would have never willingly had a man in her bed. She loves my dad. Should I call the police? No, they won't believe me. I'll call grandma. She will know what to do. I am a kid. No one will believe me anyways. I will handle this myself. I will make sure this man never touches anyone else. He will pay for what he has done."

Heavenly glances around the house for a noticeable weapon, but there is not much to use as a weapon that she can see. She stops suddenly and stares at the hallway closet. She remembers what her father told her in the case of an emergency. This is definitely an emergency to Heavenly. She goes to the closet and grabs a washcloth, like she has seen in the movies. This will keep her fingerprints from showing up at the crime scene.

She proceeds to the attic, grabs the safe, and looks on the bottom of it to get the combination as her dad had instructed her to do. She puts in the combination and gets her dad's gun. This gun is heavy for someone Heavenly's age, but she manages to pick it up. She looks admiringly at the chrome 9mm with the pearl grip and she sees her own reflection in the shiny metal. She sits on the attic floor, debating whether or not to go forward with her plan.

Meanwhile, her mom and the strange, nude guy are up in the bedroom carrying on a conversation. Heavenly is in the attic and is not aware that they are awake, and her mother is not aware that Heavenly is still in the home.

Christine gets up and approaches the man that she has in her bed. She seductively kisses him as an invite to intimacy. "I will have to tell the children about us soon. It's been almost two years and Julian no longer resides in the home. I don't want them to be caught off guard about us."

His behavior displays resistance to what she is saying.

"I don't want any hard feelings between me and the children. They may not accept their dad not being here because of our relationship."

He softly kisses Christine to assure her that he is listening, and he says, "I know what will take your mind off all those worries right now. We have plenty of time to tell them." He gestures for her to come closer to him. She slides closer to him with a bright smile on her face because she indeed likes what he has to offer. He places her gift across his chest.

She smiles and then straddles him. "You know how to make both of us happy—me and sunshine." She looks him in his eyes and says, "I'm in love, daddy," and a sarcastic chuckle follows. She then begins to passionately kiss and lick on his chest, carefully circling the gift he has offered.

Heavenly has made her way downstairs with the 9mm, struggling, but she has a grip on the gun. As she walks toward her mother's room, she has to focus on her plan. The closer she gets, she hears unfamiliar sounds that she cannot identify. She has to hurry! Her mother could be in grave danger, but she has forgotten the bullets. "Where did Dad say the bullets were?" she thinks to herself. Now she is panicking and confused about her next move. "I can't go in there with a gun and no bullets. Maybe I'll get a butcher knife from the kitchen. Maybe I'll pretend to have bullets and scare him a little bit. He should leave us alone then."

As she is deciding what to do, she hears something drop in the other room. She immediately focuses on her plan and runs to her parents' room with the gun in her hand. She busts through the door unannounced, struggling to aim the gun at the strange guy. She slowly walks toward her father's side of the bed to address the perpetrator. They haven't even noticed her presence in the room.

She gets closer and realizes her mother is on top of this man, licking his chest. She notices a white substance on his chest, and her mother is licking and smelling this strange man. Heavenly now feels such anger overcome her like she has never felt before, seeing her mom so happy with this strange man. Does her mother have something to do with her dad missing? How she could behave like this?

She holds up the gun as far up as her hands can handle and says, "Where is my dad and what have you done with him?" as her eyes tear up. She is so nervous on the inside, but seems so firm on the outside. Her mother jumps up in shock and tries to console Heavenly. The man rolls over to the other side of the bed in fear for his life.

Heavenly ignores her mother's pleas and focuses more on the nude guy. "Do not move. I have not heard your answer yet!"

Her mother is in the background crying and pleading for Heavenly to put the gun down, but she is so angry she does not hear a word her mother says. The man notices the rage in her eyes and yells out to Christine, "Please tell her who I am. I have not done anything to hurt your mother or your father."

Heavenly does not believe him. Her dad has to be dead for her mother to willingly be with another man. She just wants them to be quiet so she can think. She is so distracted from both of them pleading, she loses it and blindly pulls the trigger. When she pulls the trigger, she is blown back and thrown to the floor from the force of the gun. She misses the nude guy by a few inches from his neck, and the bullet goes into the wall. He yells and does not hesitate to grab what he can, fleeing the home in a rapid state.

Christine rushes to her daughter's aid, but Heavenly refuses the comfort and flees the home. When she gets outside there are neighbors running to her aid to make sure she is safe. Heavenly assures them she is okay and walks off in the midst of the commotion. Christine gets dressed and attempts to look for her daughter, as she is overwhelmed with confusion and hurt.

CHAPTER TWO
~ The Evolution ~

"Heavenly," is all that can be heard through the small, settled neighborhood. Christine has finally made her way out the door to search for her missing daughter, after calling Julian to come to the rescue. She quickly scans the crowd as the neighbors approach her for answers, but she ignores them as she aggressively pushes through the crowd. As she is nervously trying to think where Heavenly might have gone, her eyes come to a halt as she sees Julian standing before her.

He looks to her for confirmation of Heavenly's safety. She turns to look at the chaos she had brought into their lives. She knows none of the neighbors realize the truth of their living arrangement and she doesn't want them to find out this way. Julian walks fast and steady toward Christine because she has still not confirmed Heavenly's safety. He has a blank stare in his eyes as his focus is directly on Christine. Christine looks nervous and helpless as Julian demands to know where all his children are, especially Heavenly. She shamefully explains to him that Heavenly was the only one home and the other children are at school. She looks at Julian apologetically and asks for his forgiveness.

"Not only have you embarrassed yourself, but you now have our children caught up in your whorish cycle of entertainment," Julian says. "You better hope I find my baby girl safe and sound." He turns his back to Christine and walks away to search for Heavenly around the local neighborhood. No one notices he has tears in his eyes as he turns away from Christine. Even though he is not living at home, he still loves Christine and hates the fact that he thinks she ruined their family.

Loud and full of concern, he starts calling his daughter's name, "Heavenly. Does anyone know where my daughter could be?"

One of the elderly ladies in the neighborhood turns to him and says, "She is with those devils from around the corner."

He had many conversations with this elderly lady, so he understands exactly who she is referring to. He is now in a rage because he is aware of the types of things that go on around that specific corner. All he can think is that if someone has harmed his baby girl he will die to protect her innocence.

*****

Heavenly is unaware of all the chaos that is going on. She is eating a steak sub and watching the television. In her mind, this is so comforting. She is being catered to and treated like a child—something that she has not felt in a long time. She was so used to doing all the cooking lately, that it brought back memories of how her life used to be. They didn't even have cable anymore and it has been a long time since she has watched a live TV show. She's satisfied with the two things she had been lacking—good food and cable.

Heavenly is good friends with the neighborhood drug dealer, Reggie. He always talked about being educated, so he reminded her of her father. "What happened at your house a little while ago? Is everything okay?" Reggie asks.

She quickly speaks up and says, "I tried to kill the motherfucker who killed my dad." Reggie and other occupants of the home laugh profusely at Heavenly's answer.

"How did you try to do that, little girl?" Reggie asks.

Heavenly becomes angry because she is telling the truth and no one believes her. "I tried to shoot him with the chrome 9mm gun my father left in the closet. I missed, but if I catch him in my house or in this neighborhood, he's going to get one to the body." Her response has all of them speechless and unable to respond for a few seconds. Those were words that they would use to clarify they have beef, and here is a reflection of themselves in a young female version.

"Damn, little momma, why you so angry? I know your parents taught you better than that!"

"My dad did, but he's gone now and we were close, so I feel like I got to grow up and stop crying about this mess called life. If I don't change it, who will?"

Reggie's heart pours out to her as he looks at this beautiful, chocolate girl who just wants to be loved. He thinks of his daughter who is Heavenly's age, and cannot image being without her. He is thinking to himself that he wants to help this young lady because if his daughter was in this situation, he would want someone to embrace her too. Reggie asks for permission to sit next to her at the table, and she agrees.

*****

On the other end of the street, Julian is coming closer to the house where he suspects Heavenly could be. He already has his mind set. He will only ask one question and if there is no answer, he will not be very friendly. His only quest is to find his daughter.

He approaches the house and says a prayer. He notices no one is outside or hanging around the house, so he walks up to the door and knocks forcefully. He still doesn't get an answer. He will not leave without knowing if his daughter is in the house. He decides he is going to kick the door in, and he does just that with little strain. He kicks the door in only to discover it's the front porch to the home. He begins knocking on the second door. His knocks are so forceful they can be heard down the street, but they still go unanswered.

Julian is so determined to bring Heavenly home, he kicks the second door in. His adrenaline is rushing and he feels anxious, so he doesn't feel any of the pain from kicking both doors in. Julian doesn't care about the danger he just put himself in. All he can think about is the negativity Heavenly could be exposed to.

Julian finds himself surrounded by a lot of armed men. His hands are in the air to establish he has no weapon. "Kill me if you want to, but where the hell is my daughter?" Julian says.

"First of all, who is your damn daughter?" one of the devils asks.

Julian replies, "My daughter is Heavenly, a beautiful dark-skinned girl with shoulder length hair and she is about 4'2." After he describes her, he notices the glare in one of the devils' faces and he feels that he has found her judging by the response.

Suddenly, he sees someone come through the crowd and respond with, "That definitely is my type of chick, but she's not here, and she wouldn't be going home with you if I had her."

Julian swings at him in pure anger, only to miss. He feels a burning sensation after he hears a popping sound. His instincts tell him to fall to the ground. As he looks up, he sees one of the devils with a rifle. He is headed directly toward Julian. He wants to get up, but he is confused and feels so weak. He has another failed attempt to get up. He feels like he may lose his life, but not like this. He makes a fast decision to get up again and attempt to run out of the house. He knows this could be his last attempt to save his own life, but his attempt fails again. The devil is now standing over him, and with no remorse, aggressively hits him twice with the back of the gun. Julian passes out as his blood flows down the wooden floors of the devils' home. Everyone flees the home, not knowing or caring if he is dead or alive. They jump in the car as they take their possessions and speed out of the area, far away from the crime scene.

*****

Julian wakes up, looks around, and does not recognize any of his surroundings. He looks over to his right. There is a woman sitting next to his bed. He wants to communicate with her, but he is a little confused. She does not notice Julian is awake, or that he is attempting to communicate with her. He tries to move, but it feels like he is floating on air and he does not have control over the movement of his limbs. He pulls the tube out of his nose and the machine starts beeping. The woman notices and comes to Julian to examine him.

"Miss, what is this place? Why am I hooked to all these machines? Why is my damn mouth dry?"

She brightens the light so she can have a better sight of his health during her examination. Julian attempts to get up, but he is so weak, he immediately gives up the fight. The nurse responds to him as she examines him. "Mr. Valone, you came into the hospital about twelve hours ago. You have had major surgery and have been in guarded condition after your surgery, which is why I am here watching over you. I can give you ice chips for your dry mouth, but you cannot have anything else because you may have nausea. Please try to relax for the moment. The doctor will be in to see you shortly. If he clears you, maybe we can try to get you up tomorrow."

As she is informing Julian where he is and what has happened to him, he slowly drifts into a deep sleep. She had been slowly pumping his medicine through his veins so he could relax. She grabs her book and sits back in the chair she was in while she waits for the doctor's arrival.

*****

Reggie sits next to Heavenly. He gives her a concerned stare, looking directly in her innocent eyes. "As I look at you, I know you are a beautiful, smart, loving young lady, and it hurts my heart to see how broken you are. The streets will not fit who you are meant to be. You are different and you definitely can become whatever you put your mind to. Respect is what everyone wants. You must respect yourself in order to give someone the feeling of wanting to respect you."

As she listens to Reggie's words, she becomes sad and tears begin to steadily flow down her face as she replies, "What if I don't make it?"

He grabs Heavenly softly by the chin and says to her, "You will become whatever you choose. Make decisions that help you love life. Give whenever you can, never give up your dreams and, most importantly, pray until all these things become your reality."

Heavenly looks up slowly, feeling confused because he has touched her heart.

"What's wrong, baby girl?" Reggie asks.

"My father used to say the same things to me all the time. Now I don't know what to do. I am confused. I don't know what I must become. I wanted to be a doctor so I can take care of my parents. Now that my family is separated and my dad has been killed, I don't know who I want to be. Maybe a counselor so I can help keep families together," Heavenly says.

"You can be whatever you want to be, but never forget the neighborhood or people in it, no matter what you have accomplished," Reggie says. He gives Heavenly a hug and says, "I will be there for anything you need. I need to take you home because I know your parents are worried."

She agrees, but she dreads going home because her life is not as happy or loving at home. Reggie has made her feel like a child and she forgot how that felt. She is the mother in her home.

As they approach the corner of the street, she begins to panic. She doesn't want to go home. The street is clear and things have calmed down, but the sight of the house, which she can see clearly from the corner, gives her a weird feeling. She suddenly feels nauseated, weak, confused, and like she cannot breathe. She grabs Reggie's hand as these things are going on, then she tightly latches onto him and screams, "Lord, please help me."

Reggie quickly stops the car, jumps out, and picks Heavenly up, holding her tightly. She hugs him back even tighter, with tears in her eyes. "I don't know what just happened. I am really scared to go home."

"You must go home, for there is nothing else I can do for you right now," Reggie says. He walks to the door, carrying Heavenly in his arms. Then he knocks on the door, awaiting a response.

Christine runs to the door and sees Reggie holding Heavenly. She begins yelling, "What have you done to my daughter? Put her down."

He respects Christine's wishes and humbly says goodbye to Heavenly. "Thank you for everything," Heavenly says. She slowly makes her way into the house, as she knows she has to face the reality of today's events.

Christine grasps Heavenly and hugs, kisses, and expresses her dying love for her daughter. Heavenly pushes her away. She doesn't want to show any emotions and look weak to her mother.

Christine knows she has to fix this with her daughter, so she attempts to have a meaningful conversation with Heavenly. "Your father came here looking for you. He wanted to know you were safe. Did you speak to him or have you seen him?"

Heavenly responds, "He is alive? Where is he? Did you or that boyfriend run him away again?"

"Young lady, you need to have some respect when you speak to me. He ran off looking for you! He was upset when I called him and explained what happened. Someone said he went around the corner to the devil's house," Christine says. "Did that devil do anything to you, and are you okay?"

Heavenly replies, "They did not harm me, but what I do want to know is did you look for me?"

"No, because I knew your father was looking for you, and you are a very strong girl. I knew you would come back," Christine replies.

With her head down, Heavenly walks away from her mother's reply. She walks right out the door in an attempt to look for her father.

Heavenly starts walking around the neighborhood, asking neighbors if they've seen her father, but no one answers her. She continues walking and asking neighbors. She's sure someone knows something. She knows it will be difficult to get people to talk. That's just how her neighborhood has always been.

As she turns the corner, she runs into her best friend. He was a good kid with no guidance. Lorenzo always talked about money and the hustler lifestyle, but he never hustled. They debated all the time about who was going to be more successful, and how she was going to be his intelligent, hustling wife.

Lorenzo is walking toward Heavenly with a worried expression on his face. Heavenly knows this look very well. Something is wrong with Lorenzo, but she does not have time to talk. She has to keep walking because she has not found her father yet, so she will nicely inform him she has something very important to do right now. "Lorenzo, I can't talk to you right now. I'm looking for my father. I will fill you in later. I need to find him. I'm worried about him," Heavenly says.

"Heavenly, that's why I was coming to your house. I heard your father got shot and beaten, looking for you. He stepped to the Dirty Boys, thinking you were with them."

Heavenly instantly breaks down crying on Lorenzo shoulder, "Did they kill my dad? Where is he? Who did this to him?" Heavenly cries.

Lorenzo holds her tightly, as he feels he has deceived his friend. Lorenzo knows everything that had happened. He was the one who'd called the police and ambulance. He can't tell Heavenly he is now hustling for the Dirty Boys, and he ran after calling the police not knowing the outcome. They had promised each other not to become a product of their environment, and Heavenly will be hurt if she discovers what he knows.

"Go tell your mother what has happened. I will be here whenever you need me." He kisses her forehead and wipes her tears.

Heavenly runs home to tell her mother so they can find her father. She runs into the house, straight to her mother. "My father is dead and it's all your fault. They shot and beat him to death," she says as she falls to her mother's feet.

"Heavenly, what are you talking about?"

Heavenly responds, "Lorenzo said The Dirty Boys shot Dad because he stepped to them looking for me."

"Heavenly, we will find your father. He is not dead," Christine says as tears silently roll down her cheeks. "Get me the phonebook. I will call all the local hospitals."

CHAPTER THREE

~ The Saga ~

Lying there, looking at the ceiling, thinking about all the things that have been going on, Julian drops a tear and begins to pray to God. "Why, Lord? Why do I feel like less of a man right now? My daughter is somewhere with someone I don't know, my wife doesn't love me anymore, my other children have no clue what is going on, and I am in love with a woman who is not half the woman my wife is but I can't leave her alone. Why have you forsaken me? I left my home and kids to protect them, not to destroy them. Lord, why have I made so many bad decisions? I need you," Julian says as he lies there, wallowing in his own sorrow.

He looks up and notices the nurse approaching the door. She knocks and asks permission to come in. As she walks in, she is preparing to set up his lunch so he can eat.

"I'm not hungry," Julian says to the nurse.

"You really need to eat so we can take that walk that you spoke of a few days ago. The only way you can get better is if you follow the doctor's orders, and that means today you must start moving around. Walking is one of the requirements for you to be released. By the way, I heard you in here praying—if you call that a prayer. Stop feeling sorry for yourself and do something about it." She smiles gently and walks away. Her smile reassures Julian that this is constructive criticism, not just a criticism, so he lifts his bed up to attempt to eat his meal.

*****

As Heavenly's mother calls the area hospitals, she becomes nervous as she speaks with someone from Saint Mohawk Regional Hospital. The woman has her on hold while she looks to see if Julian is a patient. She yells for Heavenly to come in the room she is in, but Heavenly doesn't respond to her call. The woman returns to say Julian is a patient there and he is in guarded condition, but he cannot have any visitors at this time. Christine starts yelling, "He is my husband. What happened? Why we can't see him? We are his family."

"Ma'am, I cannot give you that information over the phone because I cannot identify who you are. Rest assured your husband is in great hands."

Christine drops the phone, crying hysterically and yelling, "It's all my fault. I am so sorry. Lord, please forgive me. I didn't want anyone to get hurt." She runs down the hall to Heavenly's room and finds her crying profusely on the closet floor. "Heavenly, your father is alive. We can go to the hospital to see him now," Christine says.

"I don't believe you, Mom. You have not told us the truth in so long, I really don't know who you are anymore," Heavenly responds.

"Please, Heavenly, get ready. We are going to the hospital," Christine says. As they begin to get ready to go to the hospital, Heavenly goes in the living room to find the bracelet her father gave her. As she is looking for her bracelet, she shakes the throw blanket lying across the sofa and hears her bracelet drop on the floor. She looks down on the floor and spots her bracelet. She bends down to pick it up, and notices a strange bag next to it—a small, shiny bag. She examines this bag because she does not recognize it or anything similar to it. Suddenly, Heavenly hears her name so she becomes unfocused on the bag. She puts the bracelet and the bag in her pocket in a rush to meet her mother's calls for her. They lock the doors and proceed to the hospital, which is fifteen minutes away.

While driving to the hospital, Christine feels the need to pour her heart out to Heavenly, explaining how sorry she is for everything that has happened. "Heavenly, I love you and your father, and I would not do anything to him or you. We have not been together for a while and we decided it would be best if he moved out. I love your father. He means just as much to me as you and your siblings do," Christine says with tears in her eyes, because she really does love Julian.

Heavenly sits there, looking confused. She's disgusted with her mom. "I don't understand how you love Dad, but that other man was in your bed. I also heard you doing disgusting things with that man. You obviously move on really quickly, or you don't love him," Heavenly says.

Christine replies, "We are not together, but that does not mean I don't love him. We didn't know how to tell you and your siblings that we were both seeing someone else. I have been seeing Andrew for more than a year. I didn't even know you were home. I know this is a lot to try and understand, but I really don't expect you to understand right now."

Heavenly looks out the window with a blank stare and no response. She feels so confused, frustrated, and overwhelmed with betrayal from everyone, especially her parents.

They pull into the hospital parking garage so they can find a place to park. After driving past a few rows of cars, they finally find a parking space close to the hospital entrance. They walk through the hospital to get to the reception desk to find out what floor Julian is on, and to ask if they will be able to go to the room to see him. The receptionist confirms their identity and is able to give them the room number in the ICU area. They take the elevator to the 3rd floor and ask a nurse walking by where they could find room sixteen. The nurse points them in the direction where the room is located.

Heavenly and her mother walk down the hall to the room, when they come across a security guard standing by the area they are going to. As they come closer to the room, they realize that the guard is next to Julian's room. As they approach the door to his room, the guard stops them and asks their relationship to the patient and if they have checked in at the nurses station. He explains that Julian has been violently injured and that visitors have to be authorized to see him. The guard calls the nurse who is passing by and instructs her to escort them to the desk for authorization. As the nurse is approaching the nurses station, she informs her colleagues that they are visitors for room sixteen. She informs Christine and Heavenly that they have to produce proper identification and they need to sign in. Christine gives the nurse her driver's license and Heavenly's insurance card to prove her identity.

"So, you are related to the patient, I see from the last name?" asks the nurse.

Christine replies, "Yes, his wife and daughter."

The nurse gives a look of total confusion as she states, "I don't know what is going on, but something definitely isn't right."

"May I ask why you say something is wrong? We have proper identification," Christine says.

The nurse replies, "When he was unconscious, someone came to see him. She also said she was his wife." She then radios for the security guard to come to the desk.

Christine starts yelling angrily, "I don't give damn about who lied to you, but I am legally his wife. Is he awake now so we can ask him who I am?"

Julian awakens from the noise he hears in the hallway, so he sits up and hits the buzzer for his nurse to come to his room. As he is slowly coming to, he realizes that the voice he hears sounds very familiar, but he is confused as to why she is arguing with someone in the hospital. He hits the buzzer again hoping his nurse will rush into his room and explain to him what is happening. His nurse still does not respond, but someone at the desk answers and asks if she can assist him. Julian responds by screaming, "I need my nurse in here right now."

"Someone will be in there shortly, sir. I will inform your nurse of your request," says the nurse who answered his buzz.

Heavenly is crying and upset because she has so many emotions going on, and she is confused about everything she is finding out. As Christine continues to try and convince them that she is who she says she is—his real wife—Heavenly feels faint and weak. The security guard notices Heavenly looking faint and asks Christine to calm and look after her daughter's condition before he has to escort her out of hospital. She turns rapidly to Heavenly's aid, and so does the nurse who is at the nurses station. She asks Heavenly what's wrong.

Heavenly closes her eyes and screams as she breathes rapidly, "Lord, please help me. Mommy, I don't know what is going on," Heavenly says as she falls to the ground.

The nurse assists her at the same time as she asks her questions. "Are you having chest pain, shortness of breath, or any pain?"

Heavenly answers no to all of the nurse's questions.

"I think she needs to be checked out just to be sure nothing is going on," the nurse says.

"I am okay," Heavenly says as she begins to get up from the floor.

"I have checked her vitals and she is okay, but I still recommend getting her checked out. She could just be overwhelmed from everything that is happening, but if you don't go downstairs to have her checked, please follow up with her provider," says the nurse who assessed Heavenly.

Christine agrees to the nurse's recommendation and assures her that she will take Heavenly to be checked at a later date, but for now she needs to see Julian. The security guard tells Christine he is waiting to speak with the detective and then he can clear them to see Julian. He has to follow protocol. When anyone comes in, he has to give the detective a call, but for now, she should look after her daughter and her well-being. He then walks off to call the detective and straighten things out.

"Hello, is this Detective Jean? This is the security guard from Saint Mohawk Regional Hospital, calling in regards to visitors for Julian Valone. There is currently a woman and child here claiming to be the wife and daughter of Julian, but I am puzzled. Another woman came here earlier claiming to be his wife. Did you get my message?"

Jean replies, "Yes, I did get your message. Her name is Charlene Smith, right?"

"Yes ma'am, that is correct. But this woman's name is Christine Valone and the girl's name is Heavenly Valone," the security guard responds.

"I did look up his family after you left me the message. That is legally his wife and child, but I am confused about Charlene and what her relation is to him. Try to keep them there for as long as you can. I will be there as soon as I am free."

As they hang up the phone, Jean types Charlene's name into her computer and realizes that he has the same address as she does. But he also has the same address as Christine and Heavenly.

Jean calls the security guard back at the hospital and tells him that if Charlene comes back there, to keep her close as well. She wants to know why Julian has two different addresses with two very different women. "One of these women could be the cause for Julian violently being beaten. I need to interview both of them because they are both suspects until I clear them and their alibi. Someone apparently wants Julian dead."

The security guard hangs up the phone and searches for Christine and Heavenly to inform them they can go see Julian now.

Julian has not seen anyone come to his room yet. He is distraught and desperately needs to know if that was truly Christine's voice he heard, or if he was confused because of the medication. He just wants to see Christine's face and hear her voice. He slowly sits up on the side of the bed and starts thinking about how he got in this situation. He gets some strength to try and stand to his feet, but suddenly pain starts generating through his body. He begins to lose his balance. He buckles in pain for a few seconds and then grabs a hold of the IV pole for support. Julian braces himself with the IV pole and the bed, and starts walking toward the door. He is slowly moving toward the door, but he keeps moving. He will give anything to hear that voice again. Step by step, he is getting closer to the door. He is in a lot pain and feeling weak. Suddenly he stops because he hears that voice again. This time, the voice is coming closer with every little step he takes toward the door.

As he stands there looking toward the door, he is in disbelief as to what he sees. Heavenly runs up to her father and hugs him. Christine hugs him and he can feel her face moist from tears. He hugs them both as tightly as his weak body will allow him as he, too, cries profusely. He looks up to the sky because he doesn't have the words to express his emotions.

He finally lets them both loose because his weakened body is ready to give out on him. He turns to Heavenly and says, "I am so sorry, baby. I love you and your brother and sister. I don't know the words to say, but I never wanted to be away from any of you all. I allowed me and your mother's misunderstandings to remove me out of your life. That will never happen again. I promise you, baby girl." Heavenly and her father hug each other longer and tighter this time.

Julian gives Christine a disappointed look as he hugs his daughter. A sudden sadness overcomes Christine as she watches her daughter and husband bond again. As Julian returns to the bed to rest, he says to Christine, "I am thankful that you brought Heavenly to see me under the circumstances that we are currently experiencing."

Christine looks at Julian in disbelief at his sudden kindness, but still feels some warmth in his considerate behavior because she still loves him. She replies, "No problem. We were really worried about you and didn't know whether you were dead or alive. We are relieved to know that you are alive." At that very moment, all the love and feelings she has for Julian come back. She walks out of the room as tears that she has hidden for so long come rushing down.

Heavenly sits on the side of her dad's bed and asks what happened to him. He replies, "Life happened, baby girl, and just know I will do anything to protect you and your siblings. Death won't even stop me. My spirit will always be with you."

Heavenly looks her dad in his eyes. "Daddy, if you are always going to protect us, then why was that man at our house? I had to protect us because you were not there. Where were you?"

Julian replies, "I didn't know your mother had someone in the house. I never knew she was serious enough with this guy to bring him to the house. There are going to be some changes when I get out of the hospital. I promise."

"I really thought he was hurting Mommy and that he killed you because we never seen another man in our house but you," Heavenly says.

Christine walks in the room and Julian stares at her in disgust as he says, "Heavenly, he was not trying to hurt your mother—physically anyways. She invited him in, but in the future she will be more careful to not to bring a strange man home. How did you protect your mother from this stranger?" Julian asks.

Heavenly replies, "I took your gun out of the closet and tried to shoot him like you taught me."

Julian shakes his head as he says, "No, baby. That was wrong. He was not an intruder. He was welcomed in the home by your mother. She should have explained to you all that he was going to be around now. It's not your fault. You gave your best judgment as I taught you. I love you, baby girl, but I need to talk to your mother. Go to the cafeteria and get something to eat," he says.

Christine hands Heavenly the money. Julian waits until the sound of Heavenly's footsteps disappear, so he can confront Christine.

"Christine, why would you have this man around my children?" Julian asks.

Christine replies, "Julian, you are the last person to ask any questions. You have no right to talk about who I have around the children when you left us for that whore Charlene. So, don't you dare try to judge me or what I do in the home."

"You are putting Charlene down, but what makes you any better than her? You are a married woman sleeping around with an opportunist. He is the reason you are on drugs and not taking care of your children or home, so technically, you are being the whore, Christine," Julian says.

"Julian, I have loved you for fourteen years, through the good and bad. You destroyed this family for fun and entertainment. Don't worry about what I do on my own time because you don't contribute a damn thing to my household anymore. Lust is the winner in both our lives, except you left me with your damn kids, so isn't shit now?"

"Christine, I am so sorry. I made a mistake I truly regret, but I fell for Charlene and never meant to hurt you. I still love you and we need to make it right for our kids. We just can't be in the same household anymore. Can we please get an understanding?"

Heavenly is about to walk back in the room to ask her parents if they want something, but she comes to a drastic halt and starts listening to her parents' conversation. She cannot believe the words that she is hearing; they have no respect for each other. She no longer wants to hear them argue and blame each other, so she walks in and says, "I came back to see if either of you want something, but right now I'm trying to figure out who are you two! I don't know either of you. Lies is all both of you have told, while I take care of your kids. Do either one of you want something from the cafeteria?"

Julian nods his head *no* to Heavenly's question. Christine replies, "I'll have some fries, please and thank you, baby."

"Sure, Mom. I don't think I have enough money. I may need more to get your fries."

Christine walks over to her purse to get the extra money. Heavenly reaches in her pocket to give her mother the money back. She pulls the money out and at the same time the little shiny bag and her bracelet fall on the floor. Julian and Christine look down at the bag and the whole room goes silent.

Christine rushes over to Heavenly and says, "Where did you get this, Heavenly?"

Heavenly replies, "I was looking for my bracelet that Daddy bought me and when I shook the blanket, the bag fell on the floor. I didn't know what it was, so I just put it in my pocket so I could ask what it was." Heavenly bends down and picks up the bag as Christine also reaches to pick it up. "Here,

Mother, maybe this will make you happy," Heavenly says as she hands her mother the bag of cocaine. "I want to go home now. Mark and Lindsey will be home from school real soon. It's not that either of you care anyways. I will be my own woman one day and I will take care of my brother and sister. I hate both of you," Heavenly says as she exits the room.

Julian looks at Christine in disbelief and disappointment. He starts crying profusely as he says, "Please try to fix this. Our family is so broken right now. You told me you stopped doing drugs. Apparently that was not the truth. Put the drugs down and pay attention to our kids, please. I beg you."

Christine replies, "Well, Julian, this is the only way I know how to deal with the pain of you leaving me and being in love another woman. You and Charlene can fix it, because I'm done trying to fix any damn thing that has to do with you!"

Christine storms out of the room to go find Heavenly so they can leave the hospital. Heavenly and her mother walk to the elevators and Christine says to her, "Let me explain myself, baby, because I really do love you despite everything you heard me say in there."

"I know, Mom. I'm just tired and want to go home," Heavenly says. There is nothing but silence on the way to the parking garage.

CHAPTER FOUR
~ The Regression ~

The nurse comes to Julian's room and announces herself with a knock. "I came earlier to check on you, but you were having a family discussion. The detective, Jean, is here to speak with you about how you ended up here. Is there anything you need from me before she comes in?"

Julian looks at the nurse and nods his head *no*. "Well, I will be at the nurses station. Give me a buzz if you need anything. By the way, if you start moving around more, the doctor may release you in a couple of days," the nurse states as she is leaving the room.

Julian stops her. "Miss, what if I don't want to talk to the detective?"

"It's protocol for the police to be involved when it's a violent crime, but what you want to tell them is totally up to you." Exiting the room, the nurse gives the okay for the detective to go in.

"Hello, Julian. I am Jean, a detective from the New Orleans Police Department. How are you feeling?"

Julian replies, "You being here makes me feel really uncomfortable, so get to the point and make this shit quick!"

"I don't want you to be offensive with me. I'm here to help you and your family, but I need to ask you a few questions." Jean pulls out her notepad and pen to take any information Julian gives her. "Do you know who did this to you, or have any idea who would want to hurt you or see you dead?" Jean asks Julian.

Julian replies, "First of all, lady, I didn't ask you to help me with not a damn thing. I worked hard all my life and I have never even been to jail. This shit that happened to me was unnecessary, but I don't know anything. I can't remember nothing. So please, just leave me alone and leave my room."

"Okay, Julian. You win. I will respect your wishes, but I will be watching you and your family. Here's my card if you want to grow some balls and be a man and let me know what's going on. Give me a call," Jean says.

Julian replies, "Be a man? Get the fuck out of here, dumb fucking broad." He throws her card on the floor.

Jean walks out of the room with a smirk on her face because she has seen Julian's type plenty of times—drug deals that have gone bad, getting caught with someone's woman, and many other reasons. She knows he will eventually roll over with more pressure put on him. She's just going to give him time to think about everything.

Julian turns over in the bed slowly as he starts thinking about what happened. All he can remember are the words that came out of the dude's mouth: *"Just my type of chick, and if she was here with me, she wouldn't be going home with you."* He instantly becomes furious and starts punching the bed. At that instance, he decides to get up and get out of the bed so he can get home to his family.

*****

"Heavenly, you all mean the world to me. Mommy is sick right now and I am sorry for letting you down."

Heavenly gives her mom a stern look and says, "You are a whore and we never have food. I thought whores get paid."

Christine abruptly stops and pulls over, slaps Heavenly in the face, and says, "You do not repeat what you hear when you know it's not right. I don't care how you feel. Don't ever disrespect me—now or ever."

Heavenly looks up with shame as she holds her face and says, "I am so sorry, Mommy. I only repeated it because Daddy said it and he knows you better than we do. You and him were together for a long time."

Christine looks at her daughter and starts feeling remorseful for her actions. She grabs Heavenly's hand and kisses it before she starts driving again. As Christine is driving, Heavenly, unnoticed, cuts her eyes at Christine and mumbles, "Whore" under her breath. She has a sinister smile as looks out the window and says, "Mom, we have to make it home before Lindsey and Mark get home so I can help them with their homework and cook dinner."

Christine replies, "I will make dinner and you can help with their homework."

"Okay, Mommy. We miss your cooking," Heavenly says so innocently. As they are pulling into the driveway, they notice someone at the back door. She is looking into the house. "Who is that, Mommy?" Heavenly asks.

"I don't know, but I am about to find out. Wait right here," Christine says. She gets out of the car and approaches the woman. "Can I help you? This is my home and you are peeping in my windows," Christine says to the woman.

"Hello, Christine. You have a beautiful home. I am Pamela, a caseworker from Child Protective Services. We received a call earlier today stating that there was a possibility that your kids are being neglected. If you would like, we can step inside to speak on these matters further."

Christine replies, "Lady, what the fuck you mean, I neglect my kids? Clearly, you got the wrong address."

"No ma'am, this is the right address. 275 Gross Avenue, right?" Pamela asks Christine.

"Yes, it is," Christine replies.

"Then I am at the correct address and, legally, I cannot leave until we discuss these matters. Now that you are aware of and understand my presence, would you like to invite me inside?" Pam asks as she awaits Christine's response.

"No one will be coming in my home unless I invite you. And I did not invite you." Christine yells and waves for Heavenly to come inside.

"If you don't let me in to discuss these matters, I will be forced to call the police," Pamela says to Christine.

Christine replies, "Well, you do that, and have a warrant as well."

Pamela starts walking to her car, as she wants to avoid any other conflicts. Heavenly and Christine walk into the house as they pass the CPS worker going to her car.

"Mom, you can't have the police here. I shot at the man and there are two holes in your bedroom wall," Heavenly says.

Christine responds, "You are right. Hide that gun and move my mirror over some to cover up those holes in the wall while I go get this damn CPS worker." Christine goes toward the door.

Heavenly runs to the room to move the mirror, and then she hides the gun which is still lying on the floor. She moves the mirror over and hides the gun under her mom's mattress. Heavenly then stops and prays that the woman does not take them from their mother. "Lord, please let us all stay together. I won't do anything else wrong. Amen." She walks out of the room.

Christine walks up to the car and says, "Excuse me, Mrs. Pamela, you don't need to call the police. I didn't understand how serious it was until I read your card. I am willing to cooperate and you are welcome to come in. I will be waiting inside for you."

Christine walks back to the house. As she enters, she calls Heavenly to the kitchen area. "Heavenly, where you at, baby?" Christine yells through the house.

Heavenly replies, "I am coming now, Mom." Heavenly walks in the kitchen to answer her mother's call.

"As you already know, you better not tell that woman one thing about my house. What happens in this house, stays in this house. Understood?"

Heavenly replies," I don't want her to take us, so I promise I won't say anything."

"Shh, she is coming up the driveway and about to be on the porch. Come on in, Mrs. Pamela," Christine says.

"Why isn't this young lady in school?" Pamela asks.

Christine replies, "Well, she had a doctor's appointment today and we were just coming from the doctor's office."

Pamela begins to ask a series of questions: "There are two other children mentioned in the report. Are they at school? What's your name, young lady?"

Christine replies, "The other children should be home from school any minute. Heavenly is her name and she is the oldest."

"Thank you, Christine. Heavenly, could you go in the other room while I speak with your mother, please?" Pamela asks.

Heavenly replies, "Okay, I will just go watch television."

Pamela waits until Heavenly is out of sight so she can ask Christine more personal questions. "Christine, where is your husband?" she asks.

"I don't know. We are currently separated, but he comes to visit the children on the weekends," Christine replies.

The door suddenly opens and Mark and Lindsey walk in. They both run past their mother and start yelling for Heavenly. Heavenly replies, "I am in the living room. Come in here."

Pamela notices that the children passed by their mother with no regard to her presence. She then begins to write things down on the pad. Christine gazes at her with the intent to read what is on the pad. "Christine, the children never even acknowledged your presence. Do they always ignore you?"

Christine replies, "Heavenly helps out a lot around here, especially with their father being gone, so they go to her for help with homework."

"Do you or have you ever spanked the children?" Pamela asks.

"I have spanked my children in the past, but they are going through a lot, so now I don't," Christine says, paying close attention to Pamela writing things down.

"So, in the past, what kinds of situations would cause you to spank the children?" Pamela asks.

Christine replies as she gives a long sigh, "Well, if I have to constantly ask them to behave themselves and they are not responding to my request."

Pamela continues to writes down Christine's replies, but she also jots down her body language which she notices is jittery and nervous. "Is there anyone in the home besides you and your children?"

Christine quickly looks and responds, "Of course not. It's just me and my children."

She finishes up her notes and says to Christine, "Thank you. I now need to speak to the children, so can you let me speak with them privately? You can send the young man to me. What is his name, by the way?"

"Sure, I will send Mark in here to speak with you."

Pamela gets up and follows behind Christine so she does not try to tell them what to say. Heavenly hears her mother say she will send Mark in there, so she hurries to tell Mark and Lindsey not to tell the truth to Pamela because they will be separated if she knows the truth. Pamela walks into the living room and asks Mark if it's okay for the two of them to talk alone in the kitchen. He agrees, but looks at Heavenly for permission—not his mother. Heavenly blinks her eyes twice, as this is one way they communicate without speaking. Pamela and Mark walk to the kitchen and sit at the table.

Pamela starts writing on her tablet again and Mark asks her, "Why are you writing on that notepaper?"

Pamela replies, "Well, I can't tell you or your family what to say, so I write what you tell me on this paper. Is that okay with you, Mark?"

Mark shrugs his shoulders and says, "I don't know."

"How was school today?" Pamela asks Mark.

"It was okay. We learned some more letters in cursive, we played outside, and we ate lunch."

"It sounds like you had a great day," said Pamela.

Mark replies, "I guess so."

"What do you do when you come home?" Pamela asks.

"Well, we do homework, mmm, watch TV, eat dinner, and go to bed."

"Who helps you with your homework?" Pamela asks.

Mark replies, "Heavenly is smart. She helps me and Lindsey."

"Who cooks dinner for you every day?" Pamela asks.

"Heavenly does. She is a really good cook, except macaroni and cheese; she will burn it up," Mark says as he bursts out in laughter.

Pamela smiles and tells Mark that Heavenly is a good big sister. She asks one last question. "What exactly do your mother and father do for you?" Pamela asks.

Mark replies, "Pay all the bills, sleep a lot, and I don't know."

Pamela writes down Mark's replies and says, "Thank you again, Mark. You are such an intelligent young man for your age. You have done a great job. Could you tell Lindsey to come in the kitchen so I can speak with her now?"

Mark walks away to go get Lindsey. Pamela writes on her notepad how Mark is very unsure of himself without Heavenly around to guide him.

"Hello, Lindsey. How was your day at school?" Pamela asks.

Lindsey replies, "Hi. It was okay. Why you ask me that?"

"Well, Lindsey, I just want to know how you are doing in school."

Pamela notices how Lindsey does not make eye contact with her and she seems very defensive. She decides to try a different approach with her as she asks questions. "So, Lindsey, I know Heavenly helps you with your homework every day and she cooks your dinner also. What exactly does your mother do for you?"

Lindsey replies, "She pays bills and buys a little bit of food, but Heavenly makes it stretch because she be gone to work all day and night for days at a time."

"Are you afraid when she is gone?"

"No, because my sister knows how to fight, even big people, and she always here with us every night."

"Okay, well thank you for your help, Lindsey. Can you go get Heavenly now?" Pamela makes a note about Lindsey's behavior of being shy and unable to maintain eye contact as if she is hiding something.

Heavenly walks in as Lindsey is walking out of the kitchen. She is furious from Mark's and Lindsey's responses to Pamela's questions. With a frown on her face, she pops into the kitchen chair to face Pamela. Pamela notices resistance from Heavenly and decides to let her run the show. She has been used to holding a certain power in the household and Pamela won't jeopardize that power now. That is what's been holding the family together, from what she hears and sees.

"Heavenly, is there something you want to share with me?"

Heavenly replies, "No, not really."

"Okay, how are your grades?"

"They're fair."

"Well, is there anything you and your family needs?" Pamela asks

"Sure. Everyone needs food, soap, tissues, and personal items."

"Okay, well, I will see what I can do for your family."

"Thank you," Heavenly says as she gets up from the table and goes to the living room with her siblings.

"Christine, is there anything you and your family needs?" Pamela asks.

Christine starts looking around in the refrigerator and the cabinets. "We can use a few food items."

"Well, I can see what I can do for your family." Instantly, she writes on the pad that Christine does not know anything about the children or the household. She approaches it that way so no one would know what she's doing. "Before I leave, I need to see food supply and adequate sleeping arrangements."

"Walk this way, Mrs. Pamela. This is my room." Then they walk down the hall to Lindsey and Heavenly's room. Across from their room is Mark's.

"I know you are a very busy woman, but your house is very clean for three children. Do the children help keep the house clean? Like chores?" Pamela asks.

"Heavenly usually helps me clean up and tidy the house every night before bed. She loves a clean house," Christine says. As they walk back to the kitchen, Christine opens the refrigerator and freezer and says, "There is not much in there, but I am going to the store later."

Pamela replies, "If you would like, I will bring you a voucher tomorrow evening, but for now it is enough."

"Thank you, Mrs. Pamela," Christine says.

Pamela responds deceitfully, "You are welcome, Mrs. Christine. It looks like you are doing a great job. You will receive a notice in the mail stating our findings. The case will stay open for sixty days unless we have found you falsely accused." Pamela leaves and she feels something isn't right, but by law, she can only document her objective not subjective findings.

Christine walks into the living room, looks at the children, and says, "This is why he should have taken you all with him and his little bitch. Heavenly, you are a replica of your father—just plain out fucking evil." She walks away.

Heavenly's feelings are hurt, but she won't show any emotions or weakness as she asks, "Mom, are you cooking dinner tonight?"

"Hell no. I am about to leave. You cook with your grown ass," Christine replies.

"Okay, Mom," she says. Heavenly tells Lindsey and Mark that after she makes dinner, she is going to leave for a little while, so she wants them to watch TV until she returns. She finds two cans of spaghettios in the cabinet. She opens them and puts them in the microwave to be warmed and served. Heavenly calls Lindsey and Mark to come eat dinner and she says to them, "Remember what I told you. Eat and then go in the living room." She kisses them on the forehead and heads out the door.

*****

Julian hears the phone ring. He looks at it, then answers. "Hello."

"Hi, baby. How are you feeling?" says the voice on the other end of the phone.

"I would be better, Charlene, if you were here with me. You only came here once."

Charlene replies, "You know I love you, but I thought maybe your children and other family members were coming. If you need me, I will be there tomorrow."

Tears start rolling down Julian's eyes as he says, "I left my wife to be with you. I just wish you would support me more. I don't feel loved by you with the things you say sometimes."

"First of all," Charlene says, "you left because you weren't happy, not just to be with me. I will compromise with you, but I will not stop my life because you are in your feelings. I will be going out with my friends tonight and I will see you tomorrow."

"I never asked you to change your life, but what happened to the affection and love you used to show me?" he asks.

"Julian, you are around me all the time. Why would I miss you like I used to?"

"Wow, Charlene. After all that we been through, you still have no compassion for me."

Charlene replies before she hangs up the phone. "I am not about to argue with you. Take it or leave it. Bye. See you tomorrow."

Julian is feeling lost and confused, now questioning his actions. When did Charlene stop loving him? How could she not love him? She'd chased him for years and now that she had him, she clearly doesn't care about him. But he truly still loves her. With the news he got earlier today and Charlene acting nonchalant, he is overwhelmed. All Julian knows is that in two days, he will be out of the hospital and he has some major decisions to make. His life is out of order in every direction. He gets up and attempts to walk around the room on his own. He no longer wants to patiently wait for the nurse. He has unfinished business on the outside.

*****

Heavenly walks down the street on a mission to get a couple dollars for food. She knows exactly where to go. There is no brainstorming on this one. Walking slowly, she is thinking of a way to ask Reggie for some money. She knows he looks at her as a daughter, but she looks at him as a bank that asks her for nothing. She is in her train of thought, walking toward Reggie's house, when she vaguely hears her name. The more steps she takes, the louder it gets.

"Heavenly."

"What Lorenzo? I'm on a mission. What's up?"

"Yo, my mom said the CPS people was at your house. You good?"

"Of course, stupid. I know how to talk to those people."

"Well, with your mom always being gone, you think they going to find out?"

"No, I just won't open the door."

Lorenzo laughs. "You swear you grown. I like that, though. Did you find your pops and is he okay?"

"Yes, he is okay. But go on ahead, little boy. I got something to do."

"Alright, then. Call me later."

They slap up and part ways. Lorenzo is wondering how much she knows about what happened to her dad, and for thirty seconds, he considers telling her.

*****

Heavenly knocks on Reggie's door and announces herself.

"Heavenly." Reggie's homeboy opens the door and invites her in.

"Who is that at the door?" Reggie asks.

"It's your daughter from another mother," says his friend.

"Heavenly," he replies. He comes down the stairs and greets her with a hug and a smile. "Have you been going to school? And do not forget, I want to see that report card."

"Yes, I have, but not today of course." Heavenly puts on a sad look because she knows Reggie will ask her what's wrong. She says, "Remember you said if I need anything to come to you and don't do anything stupid?"

Reggie replies, "Yes, baby girl. What's wrong? What do you need?"

Heavenly replies, "Well, CPS came to our house and they're going to take us if we don't have any food. I don't want to go to no foster system."

Reggie replies, "How much do you need and who's going to take you to the store?"

Heavenly replies, "I don't know how to shop and my mom's car isn't working good. Can you take me?"

Reggie replies, "Hold on, baby. Anything for you. Let me get my keys."

At that point, Heavenly is excited that Reggie is buying groceries, but she wonders if she can get more than groceries. She's seen on TV how women are always getting what they want from men and she wants to learn how to do that because she has a different feeling around Reggie. She feels protected and loved, like when she is with her father.

"Let's go get these groceries so you can get home and get ready for school."

"Thank you so much," Heavenly says and she kisses Reggie on the cheek.

They arrive at the grocery store and Reggie says to Heavenly, "Get whatever you all need—soap, tissue, anything. I got you."

Heavenly walks down the aisle and starts picking up a lot of junk food, but she realizes they cannot survive on junk food, so she starts to put things back. Reggie stops her and says, "No, we will get the real food."

Heavenly just smiles at him with intent to melt his heart. As they finish shopping and approach the register, she hears someone calling Reggie's name. He turns to see who is calling him. As Reggie is laughing and giggling with this female friend, Heavenly angrily waits and she doesn't understand why she has this feeling. She does not know that woman. Heavenly sees the way she flirts with Reggie and it is making her mad. Is Reggie naïve, or just dumb? She watches as Reggie gives the woman some money, kisses her on the cheek, and watches her walk away. This has Heavenly curious as to why would he be so generous. All she sees is someone in heels about to break her hips if she walks any harder—nothing exciting about her.

They begin to cash out and walk toward the door when Reggie sees one of his homeboys. "What's up, my dude? How you been?" the friend says.

Reggie replies, "Man, making this money, trying to make business moves and bless others, living life. Thanks for asking, though. How are you?"

The friend replies, "Taking care of my family. Struggling, but we making it though. Well, let me get these groceries before the wife start tripping." He laughs. They slap each other up.

"Alright, man. See you later."

The friend yells as he is walking away, "Yo Reggie, you volunteering at the church Sunday?"

"Fa sho," Reggie replies, and they both continue to walk away.

Heavenly is confused how a known drug dealer is respected at church. These were bad people as far as she knew, but there was something different about Reggie. They put the bags in the car and begin the ride home.

"Can I ask you a question?" Heavenly asks.

Reggie replies, "Sure, anything you want to know."

Heavenly begins to ask questions. "How come if you into church, you don't have a wife and you sell drugs?"

"Well, baby girl, you can be doing time without going to jail. I will be free one day soon."

"I don't understand. You went to jail? You on probation?"

"No, neither of those fit me, but when you start doing your time, you will understand. For now, be a kid and stop being so grown up, okay?"

"Okay, Reggie."

They pull up to the house and Heavenly notices her mom's car is not in the driveway. "Thank you, Reggie. I will take the bags in. I don't want my mom to come and find you in the house."

Reggie grabs the bags as he says, "That's a man's job to help his daughter and his lady, and you're like a daughter to me. So I will help you get these groceries in the house."

Heavenly gives Reggie the rest of the bags she has in her hands and says, "Okay, Reggie. If you insist."

They walk into the house with the groceries. Mark and Lindsey glance at them as they enter the kitchen, and then continue to watch TV. Reggie notices the children are there with no grown up and begins to question Heavenly. "Where are your parents?"

Heavenly replies, "My dad is in the hospital and my mom is at work. We will be fine until she gets home. She always works late hours."

Reggie grabs Heavenly's hand and says, "You can tell me if your parents are not treating you and your siblings right. I will keep you in my prayers because I know you are protecting your parents. Let's pray right now. Bow your head as we pray: *God protect these children day and night, make a covenant to keep them safe from anything or anyone that could harm them. Amen.* Lock this door until your parents come home," Reggie says.

Heavenly agrees with Reggie, not knowing when her mother will return home.

She orders Lindsey and Mark to take showers while she puts up the food. Heavenly has grown very fatigued from this overwhelming day. She just wants to go to bed and forget this day exists. She puts up the food and sits on the couch, waiting for Mark to finish his shower so she can get in and go to bed. Heavenly says her prayers with Lindsey and yells for Mark to hurry out of the bathroom. He finally comes out and she directs him to say his prayers and go to bed too.

Heavenly finally gets in the shower and all that has happened today is flowing through her mind. All of a sudden, she has this strange feeling overcome her. She feels different, nervous, jittery, and she forgets where she is. Her vision is blurry and she is breathing heavily. She is so confused, she falls on the shower floor, closes her eyes, and yells, "God, please help me. I don't know what is going on."

As she starts to open her eyes, her vision becomes much clearer. She doesn't know what happened, but it was very scary. She continues to take her shower. She gets out of the shower, dries herself off, and puts her clothing on. She goes around the house and starts dimming the lights in the home, so it looks like someone is home. As Heavenly gets ready for bed, she says her prayers. She asks God to help her with her life.

71

And she is confused about why she feels different around Reggie.

*****

Christine and Andrew pull up to the house around the corner to go get their fix for the night. Christine approaches the house. It looks dark and vacant, but she notices someone walking up to her. Andrew gets out of the car when he sees someone coming from the side of the house. He notices it is Slim, so he slaps him up.

Slim asks Andrew if he is with Christine. Andrew nods his head yes. Slim says to Andrew, "We need a new spot. You think she will know someone or somewhere I can conduct my business?"

Andrew replies, "You can ask her when she gets what she needs. I'm about to go back to the car, but I'll holla."

Christine walks toward Slim and Andrew as they slap up and finish their conversation

"What can I do for you, momma?" Slim asks.

"I need three. You know ya'll got the best shit around here," Christine replies.

Slim replies, "Listen, I appreciate you and all your business, but we will no longer be working from here."

"Well, where will I find you?"

"I don't know. I'll be around unless you know somewhere for me to work from."

Christine replies, "What do I get if I can find you a place?"

"I'll supply your needs if you supply mine," Slim says.

"I have the perfect place for me and you to do business. Come by my house tomorrow morning around 10:00 AM and we can talk," Christine says.

"Bet it up. I will see you then. Here goes another bag for helping me out." Slim walks away and Christine gets back in the car with Andrew.

"I paid for three and he gave me an extra one," Christine says excitedly.

"Tell me what you think about this. He needs a spot and I was going to set up a meeting so he can talk to you about doing some business. He'll give us all the supplies for free and he will keep groceries there for you to cook every day," Andrew says.

Christine replies, "Well, I know two dudes that have the same hustle won't make it. That is a disaster waiting to happen."

"That's why you are going to bring the business to your house. More control for me. They are all from around the neighborhood and you can be home more with the children. I will be at your house every day Everything you need is in one spot." He reaches over and passionately kisses her on the lips.

Christine says, "You are right, baby. You can set it up for us to meet tomorrow, but for now, I need to get this fix. You know how this shit makes me freaky."

"I love you, Christine. Thank you for trusting me, baby."

"I love you more, Andrew."

Andrew and Christine drive away to get their night started.

*****

Morning arrives as Christine heads home to see if her children went to school. She arrives at her home to find it empty. Everyone has gone to school. It is now 8:00 AM and she has two hours before she meets with Slim. She decides to lie down as she has been up all night with Andrew. She stumbles to her room and drops on the bed. Within seconds she is out cold.

Christine hears someone faintly calling her name. She gently moves, as she thinks she is dreaming. Suddenly, the calling of her name becomes louder and she jumps up out of her sleep.

Slim is standing over her with a wicked smile on his face as he says, "Did you forget about our meeting this morning?"

Christine replies, "No, of course not. I am awake now. Could you go in the kitchen and wait there for me to get up and get dressed?"

Slim turns around and walks toward the kitchen as he laughs and says, "You can get dressed. I have seen plenty of women's bodies."

Christine shakes her head and gets up to get dressed. She is feeling nauseated and confused from her hangover. She walks in the kitchen and sits at the table where Slim is already awaiting her presence.

Slim sits up in his chair, looks at Christine, and says, "So, let's talk business. Where is the spot you have for me?"

Christine replies, "Me and Andrew decided you can do it right here, but you can't have all your friends hanging around my house. I have daughters. I just ask you to respect that one condition, or the deal is off."

Slim replies with a smirk on his face, "I definitely understand. I will respect your home. You are helping me by inviting me into your home. Thank you. We will be setting up for a couple of days. Here are a few supplies for you while I get things situated. Don't use it all in one place." He shakes Christine's hand as a gesture that their business is done and they are in agreement.

Slim picks up his cell phone as he walks out the door and makes a phone call, "Yo, the plan is definitely in operation. I'm a holla at you later, my dude." He disconnects the call and smiles in great pleasure, as he continues his day.

Christine grabs the supply Slim left and calls Andrew, "It's done, baby. I got you for a few days and you know I will be over tonight. Love you."

CHAPTER FIVE

~ The Ending to a New Beginning ~

"Yo, dude. Put that camera up on the roof by the front of the house, because that camera turns in three directions," Slim says.

Slim goes back in the house to finish setting up the security system. "Where can I set this up so I can always see who is coming in and out of the house?" Slim asks.

Christine replies, "You can set it up on the side of the entertainment stand so it won't be in the children's way when they walk through the living room."

"Cool. I will need to see all your heater vents, and by the way, does the ceiling fixture move if you touch it?"

"No, it doesn't, but why do you need to know if it moves?" Christine asks.

"Let me tell you something right now," Slim says. "You ask too many fucking questions and if my shit comes up short or missing, I will kill your whole damn family. So don't ask me nothing about how I move, just do what I ask, stupid ass woman."

The look Slim has in his eyes while he speaks to Christine makes her extremely nervous so she responds immediately. "Okay, I won't ask you any more questions about your business."

Slim says, "Here's some money. Go to the store, get me some liquor, and cook some breakfast when you return. A motherfucker going to be hungry from doing all this damn work."

Christine immediately grabs the money and gets ready to make the store run for Slim.

*****

"Well, Julian. Today is your big day. You will be released in a few hours. Oh, by the way, the detective will be here shortly to speak with you," the nurse says to Julian as she walks out of the room.

Julian sits up on the side of the bed thinking about everything that has happened. He is so lost in his thoughts, a tear drops without him realizing what is happening. As he wipes his tears, he says, "This too shall pass."

He picks up the phone to call Charlene so she can pick him up from the hospital. "Baby, I will be released in a little while. I can't wait to see you and get in my own bed under your warm body."

He notices there is an awkward silence, so he pauses before Charlene begins to say with no emotion, "I will be there in an hour, Julian."

She hangs up the phone. She has a few thoughts that the conversation with Julian stirred up along with her emotions. She says out loud, "How will I tell him I no longer want this relationship? I thought I was still in love with him, but I realize I am not feeling him. Oh well. Let me get dressed and go get this corny ass dude." Charlene gets dressed and heads to the hospital to get Julian.

*****

The detective knocks as she enters the room and says, "Hello again, Julian. I see you are getting released today. Is there anything you would like for me to know?"

Julian gives Jean a blank stare and then turns to look out the window as he replies, "I don't speak on things that I don't have the facts on what happened, so you're wasting your time, lady."

Jean replies, "This is my job. Helping someone get justice is a lifestyle for me. If they did this to you, it's apparent they want you dead. Please understand when you leave here, I can't protect you if you won't let me." She drops her card on the table and begins to walk away. She stops suddenly and says, "I will see you again, whether face to face or viewing your body at a crime scene. Your choice, team player."

*****

Charlene arrives at the hospital and a sudden emotion of sadness has overcome her thoughts. She looks in the rearview mirror and starts speaking to herself as she says, "Girl you can do better than this. Julian is a good dude, but he is from the past. You said you would never go backwards. Besides he has done nothing but hurt you. He is married and he left her—you won't be different. Get rid of him. He is just a rebound from Mike." She fixes her hair, takes a deep breath, and exits the car.

As Charlene is getting off the elevator, Jean is standing there getting ready to get on. Jean recognizes Charlene, but doesn't know from where. "Hello, my name is Jean and for some reason you look really familiar. Do I know you?"

"I don't think I know you," Charlene says.

"I remember faces, not names, and you look familiar to me. I apologize, but it was nice meeting you," Jean says.

Charlene exits the elevator and Jean enters with a puzzled look because she definitely knows Charlene from somewhere. She says out loud, "I'll figure out where I know her from. It will hit me later.

*****

"Here is your paperwork to sign. In three days, call your primary care physician and make a follow-up appointment. Here is your script for pain and your antibiotics for several days to make sure there is no infection. Sign here, stating I gave you discharge instructions." She stops Julian before he goes out the door and says, "Julian, I really think you are a very nice person. Don't let what happened to you define you. You are alive and that means you have a purpose here.

You are somebody, but only you can define what kind of somebody you want to be. Take care of yourself and that beautiful daughter of yours."

Julian signs the papers as he cracks a smile, relieved to be getting out of the hospital. "Thank you, ma'am. It's been bittersweet in this place, but you helped me get through it."

As she reaches over to give Julian a friendly hug, she notices someone standing in the doorway. "Hello, I was his nurse during his stay. Are you here to pick him up?" the nurse asks.

Charlene walks past the nurse to get to Julian. She does not say a word to her. "Julian, I see you are being a whore as usual. You fucking her too?" She rolls her eyes in disbelief he is hugging the nurse.

Julian replies, "Charlene, I am not messing with that woman. I love you. Don't you see that?" He holds his head down in disbelief of Charlene actions.

Charlene replies, "Well, you said you loved me then, but what stopped you from hurting my feelings? I believe you could be a pro by now." She laughs the seriousness away.

"Could you grab my bag and I can wheel myself out?" Julian asks as he ignores Charlene's cries for negative attention. All he thinks about are his kids and how he is going to find those guys who did this to him.

"Do you need help getting in the car?" Charlene asks.

"No thank you," Julian says. He gets in and closes the door, then turns to Charlene and says, "Thank you."

"Sure," Charlene says.

As they are riding along the streets of New Orleans, Julian starts reflecting on his life which was great and stable for a long time, but for the last eighteen months, he did not know what was going to happen from day to day.

"Charlene, you know I love you, but I can't deal with your negativity. Please just look at all I have done to prove to you I am here for you. I know what I did in the past, but I am trying really hard now. Give me a chance," Julian says.

Charlene starts breaking down and feeling remorse for her behavior. She turns, looks at Julian, and says, "I do love you, but I have been through a lot which makes me put up my guard. I want to love you, but I have to learn how to again. I am not in love with you. I thought I was, but I have love for you. I'm so sorry."

These words hit Julian like a knife. He had completely left his family two years ago to be with her, and now she doesn't love him like he loves her. "It's cool, Charlene. I wish you would have said that before I made the major move. You bitches are all alike."

"Julian, don't disrespect me like that. When did you start talking to me like that?"

Julian angrily replies, "When you fucking ruined my life."

Charlene becomes very upset as she replies, "I just wanted someone to comfort me. You made a mistake and confused me. I never told you to leave your family, but you did, Furthermore, I was having fun. I just got out of a relationship with Mike and I told you we were moving too fast. You never listened to me, so here we are today. So, don't throw your guilt trip on me. Take responsibility for your actions."

As they are pulling up to the house, Julian sheds a tear as he says, "No one should live in misery, and I promised to make you happy again. Thank you for everything. I really appreciate you." He grabs his crutch, gets out of the car, and walks toward the house. Charlene walks behind him with his bags.

*****

"Slim, I got your liquor and, by the way, I kept the change," Christine says.

"That's cool. Could you please go cook me and my dudes some breakfast now?"

"Sure what do ya'll want to eat?"

"Whatever you got in there that can fill us up." Slim and his boys proceed to playing the PlayStation.

Christine walks away toward the kitchen. She pulls out the pots and pans and begins to put breakfast together. As she stares in her living room at Slim and his boys, she starts to daydream about Julian and the kids sitting there having a good time playing board games. Christine feels a sudden sadness overcome her and says out loud, "How did it come to this?" She comes to and continues to cook.

"Slim, does she know anything yet?" Andrew asks.

Slim replies, "Do your fucking part. Keep fucking the broad and she won't know nothing unless you tell her. Are you falling in love with this broad? Because you acting just like her, asking all these damn questions."

Andrew replies, "Hell naw, dude. You know how I move. It's business, never personal."

Slim replies as he laughs hysterically, "Cool, then play the game so I can spank that ass, dude."

"How long before the food is done, Christine? And what time the children comes home, baby?" Andrew asks.

Christine sarcastically replies, "Bae, the food will be done real soon and the kids come home around 3:30 PM. Why, are you going to help with their homework?"

Andrew replies with a seductive smile on his face, "Sure, I will help. Not sure what I can help with, but you got some homework to do before they get home. This homework requires you to do a lot of thinking and no writing, but you can do it with no hands."

Christine doesn't reply because she knows that is his code for a blow job, so she just smiles back at him. "Brunch is served. You all can fix your own plates," Christine says as she walks toward her bedroom with her plate in her hand.

Slim, Andrew, and some of the Dirty Boys head to the kitchen to eat. Everyone makes their plates and proceeds to the living room. Slim looks at Andrew and a sudden thought comes across his mind. He turns to Andrew and says, "I really need you focused and keeping this woman in line. Christine needs to believe and trust everything you say and do. The reason I am saying this is because you really look happy to be messing with this broad. Stay focused, my dude, or there will be problems for you instead of her."

Andrew knows that Slim is a dangerous man, so he is cautious about his response because he does care about Christine. Andrew replies, "Man, you know me. I don't let these broads get to my heart. That's against the player's anthem."

Slim replies, 'I hope so because it will get real ugly, my dude."

*****

Julian sits on the couch and begins to roll his blunt. He doesn't smoke on the regular, but when things get rough for him, he smokes to relax. Charlene has been smoking since they were younger, so she is always ready to smoke.

"You ready to smoke, Charlene? I'm almost done rolling this blunt." Julian says.

Charlene replies, "Hell yea. Where you at? In the living room? Here I come right now." Charlene comes into the living room and sits next to Julian on the couch.

As they are smoking, Julian starts thinking about his children as he says, "When my kids get out of school, I am going over to the house and see them. I really miss seeing them every day."

Charlene looks at Julian with a smirk on her face and says, "I knew that much. It is definitely evident you miss your children."

Julian replies, "Yo, Charlene, don't blow my high with all that smart mouth bullshit. Keep it to yourself. I'm trying to relax, so just chill. What you can do is give me some pussy before I leave."

As Charlene is looking at Julian while he is talking to her, she is wondering how she is going to give him the best sex they ever had because he deserves it for this last time. She loves it when Julian talks to her with authority; he is sexier to her when he takes charge. Charlene replies with a big smile as she says, "I can definitely do that. I miss you anyways, Big Daddy."

Julian puts out the blunt and stares at Charlene. She notices Julian staring at her in a seductive way, so she stands up in front of him, bends down, and passionately kisses him on his lips. As she is standing over him, she pulls his head close to her stomach as she gently rubs his head. He rests his head on her stomach as a sign of submission. She slowly grabs his hand and kisses it with her moist, but soft lips, as she is showing him her submission. As he begins to slowly get aroused, he grabs her by her inner thighs, pulling her closer to him. She wants to feel the warmth of both of his hands, so she guides his hands to her waist. She slowly slides their hands down to her buttocks as they both grasp it together. She bends over closer to him as she presses her big breasts into his face and says, "Let's go to the room, Daddy. I got something special for you today."

She helps him to the bedroom and undresses him as well. He sits on the side of the bed as he watches Charlene seductively get undressed. She turns around fully undressed, looks into his eyes as she approaches him, and slowly pushes him back onto the bed as she straddles him. She begins to passionately kiss him as she guides his hands to her buttock. She slowly sits straight up on top of Julian as she begins to manipulate her breasts with her hands while he watches.

Julian watches her manipulating her breasts and joins her as he becomes more aroused. He loves the way her breast feels. He wants to have a taste of them, so he begins manipulating her breast with his tongue. Charlene is enjoying Julian's tongue manipulation, so she begins to moan and gyrate her hips on his mountain of love. He picks her up and gently lays her on her back as she wraps her legs tightly around his nicely figured waist. He slowly and gently kisses her lips as he stares at her. He rubs her feet with his hands and she holds her leg up for more. He slowly kisses her foot with his beautiful, full lips. She stares at him with deep lust as she moans for more.

He is slowly working his way up to her love box. As he reaches her love box, he sits his soft lips right there. She feels the warmth of his lips and his heavy breathing on her love box and she arches her back so he can give her more. His lips rest on her love box and he begins to massage her inner thighs softly as he slowly spreads them at the same time. She becomes so moist his lips are glazed with her passion. As he has her legs spread, he looks into her eyes as he begins to softly lick on her clitoris.

Charlene has a sudden, uncontrolled shake flow through her body as he continues to lick and kiss her clitoris. He notices her reaction to what he is doing, so he begins to gently suck on her clitoris as he is massaging her outer thigh. She is so full of passion, she releases a water fountain of love. Julian uses his tongue to saturate up all of her juices. He doesn't stop because he knows she is near her highest peak, so he starts sucking and licking her box until she can't take it anymore. She is now trembling and breathing heavily until she busts. Now she is pulling away and Julian is pulling her back until she begs for him to stop. He stops, comes up, and faces her, kissing her passionately as he slides his mountain of lust inside of her.

They both moan as a sign of pleasure, as their pelvises thrust with the same rhythm. Julian gently grabs her throat to show her he is in control. The motion of sliding in and out of her love box has him in a daze. He looks at Charlene as he loves to see her totally submissive, so he kisses her again as his mountain of love fills up her love box. All he feels is warmth and moisture which has his mountain pulsating and ready to create life. He passionately stares at her as he's sliding in and out of her love box and says, "I love you."

Charlene replies seductively, "I love you too, Daddy." Her response sends him over the edge as he rapidly slides in and out, and starts trembling until he has released fruitfully in her love box. He stops to catch his breath as he is still inside her. He slowly begins to slide out of her love box and then lies next to her.

*****

"Baby, I am ready for you to do your homework," Andrew says with a chuckle.

Christine smiles at Andrew, standing in the doorway as she says, "I have been ready. Come in here so you can help me. I know you need tutoring too."

Andrew enters the room and shuts the door so they can have some privacy. Christine goes to her dresser drawer and pulls out two bags of cocaine and a mirror. Andrew comments as she brings out the cocaine and mirror, "You know how freaky I get when I have some of that good shit. I can't wait to slide up in that waterfall."

They both do a line each. As they let it settle, they turn and stare at each other with their eyes full of lust. Christine puts the mirror and supplies on the dresser and walks back to the bed where Andrew is sitting. Christine and Andrew began to kiss so passionately, they take deep breaths between each kiss. As they look into each other's eyes, it is getting hot between her rays of sunshine and as he slowly gets aroused. He undresses Christine and quickly takes his clothes off as well. He climbs back on the bed between her rays of sunshine. Not only does he feel the heat from her sunshine, he feels the moisture from the coming of the rain that's about to pour on his pole as he presses against her. He is at full attention while he is gently biting and sucking on her breast. She moans for him to give her more.

Andrew grabs his pole and guides it slowly into her sunshine as he says out loud, "Oh my god." He is mentally in another place with the heat and moisture from Christine's sunshine. She closes her eyes to focus on the movement of his pole, so she can figure out his rhythm. He notices her eyes are closed, so he slides out gently and back in forcibly, so she knows he is in control. He speeds up the pace of his strokes and as she accepts his aggressive strokes, she willingly opens her sunshine into a V shape so he can have unlimited access to her universe. He slows his strokes down because he might bust too quickly due to the way she changed the position of her pelvis.

He grabs her legs and pushes them back as he holds tightly to one thigh. He slides in and out of her sunshine while looking at his pole and watching her rubbing her clitoris. She is getting more turned on, so she grasps her breast with her free hand and gently rolls her tongue around the tip of her nipples. Andrew is getting excited again and is sweating profusely as he starts going faster.

Christine screams, "Yes, Daddy. Get this pussy." She releases the grasp on her breast and slides her finger in and out of her mouth as if it was his pole. Andrew notices her actions and slows down as he slides out of her sunshine.

Christine begins to lick up and down his pole, and then gently on the top of it as he moans in lust. Her soft lips and her unique strokes with her tongue send him over the edge. Christine looks at Andrew with his pole in her mouth and says, "No, Daddy. Not yet. I'm not done."

He closes his eyes so he focuses on something else because he doesn't want to prematurely bust. Christine suddenly stops because she knows Andrew will bust quickly if she continues. She aggressively pushes Andrew on the bed, then she climbs on top of him and slides down his pole. Already on the edge, Andrew jerks from the sudden warmth and moisture of her sunshine. She slides up and down his pole rapidly in a soft bounce. As she begins to get more into it and arch her back, she places her hands on his chest for support so he can fill all of her sunshine. She is working her back so that her buttocks land on his sack of love every time she slides back down his pole. She knows she is in control and shows no mercy because she knows the friction from her motion will drive him crazy. As she wildly slides up and down his pole, he wants to be deeper inside her, so he grabs both sides of her thighs and assists her with her strokes.

She is so focused on how good it feels, she relaxes her head in order to keep the position she is in and goes faster as she feels the rain about to pour down as Andrew says, "I'm about to cum, baby. I'm sorry."

"Christine softly replies, "Me too, baby."

She squeezes her pelvis as she feels his throbbing, and the rain begins to pour on top of his pole. He grabs the pillow to silence his moans of lust. He is shaking in disbelief as she sits there trying to catch her breath. She climbs off his pole and lies on his chest, both of them breathing heavily.

*****

Meanwhile, Charlene stares at Julian and gently kisses him on the lips as she says, "Julian, I am so sorry, but I am not in love with you anymore. I deeply care for you, but not enough to stay in this relationship. What we have is very special and you will always have a place in my heart, but we are on two different pages."

Julian replies with tears in his eyes, "I totally agree with you. I'm sorry I couldn't be what you needed me to be, and I have failed you a second time. Just know my love for you will always be here. Thank you for the opportunity to get to know you all over again."

Julian sits up on the side of the bed as he puts his clothes on, turns, and looks at Charlene. With his eyes full of tears, he says, "I really do love you."

Charlene looks at Julian with sorrow. There are tears in her eyes as well as she says, "I love you more."

They hug each other tightly for a few minutes and both refuse to let go. Julian kisses Charlene on the forehead before he releases her and then walks to the bathroom. As he is in the bathroom washing up, he looks up at himself in the mirror. He has now decided leaving his family was a big mistake. He has always loved Christine. She means everything to him. As he goes into the bedroom to get dressed, he looks at Charlene and he regrets this whole situation.

He leaves the room and walks toward the living room to gather his coat and keys. He says to Charlene, "When I return it would be in your best interest not to be here. I would appreciate it if you and everything you own is gone. Thank you." He walks out the door to go see his children and his wife, hoping he can reconnect with his true love and his children.

Charlene lies in the bed crying because she is not sure if her decision was right. It doesn't feel right and, furthermore, she hasn't taken the pregnancy test yet.

*****

Slim and his boys are sitting in the living room of Christine's house playing the game and drinking. He notices his drink is low and says, "That food was great, but my drink is running low. I can't send that broad because she and Andrew lay-up, boo loving. Any of you dudes want to go to the store with me? I'm getting some more liquor." Slim and a few of the Dirty Boys walk out the door toward his car.

CHAPTER SIX

~ The Hustle ~

Julian starts the car and suddenly feels overwhelmed, so he begins to pray. "Lord, I have made so many mistakes and hurt so many people, but I never intentionally hurt anyone. Please forgive me for my actions, Lord. Whatever is your will, I will receive it. Please can I have my family back? I promise to be faithful and obey your word. In Jesus's name, I pray. Amen."

Julian pulls up to his home where Christine and his children reside. He sits in the car, takes a deep breath, and closes his eyes to relax. As he exits the car, he is thinking he should have brought her some flowers, but he knows Christine will be thankful for his presence.

He starts walking toward the house and he hears someone screaming, "Daddy." So he looks around to see where this voice is coming from. He looks down the street to see that it is his daughter, Heavenly. They run to each other and have a long, tight hug. They both look up as they hear a screeching sound, and they notice it is the school bus. As the bus comes to a stop, Mark and Lindsey exit the bus and run toward Julian and Heavenly. They all hug each other so tight, with tears in their eyes and many questions on the tips of their tongues. They continue to hug for a long time and repeatedly say, "I love you, Daddy."

Julian looks down at all his children and says to them, "Daddy is home for good now. I will never leave you all again. We need to go in the house and let your mother know you all are home," Julian tells the children.

They walk to the house. Each one of them is full of joy. It has been a long time since the family felt complete. As they continue to walk to the house, Julian explains to the children, "There has been trouble in this family, but I am here now and I am now focused on what is important—us being together as a family."

Julian opens the door to let his children in as he yells for Christine. There is no answer to his calls, so he tells the children to go in the living room while he talks to their mother who could be asleep. Julian is thinking that he has a lot to do for the family. The drugs have consumed Christine. He truly loves Christine and he's sure of it, just like the day he married her. He will do whatever it takes to fix this for his family. He walks down the hall to the bedroom so he can talk to Christine.

Meanwhile in the living room, Heavenly and her siblings are excited and talking to each other. Heavenly says to Mark and Lindsey, "Dad is back for good now. That means we must behave. We don't want to give them any more problems than they already have. We should do something nice for them. Maybe we can cook dinner for just the two of them, or they can go out and we can clean up really good by the time they come back."

Just as Heavenly is talking to her siblings, they hear a car door slam and people talking really loud, as if they were in their driveway. Heavenly goes to the window to see who is in the yard, only to realize it is a couple of the Dirty Boys. Heavenly knows something isn't right. Why would they be coming to her house?

Heavenly moves away from the window to go meet them in the yard. She runs into some of their video surveillance and she says, "What is this stuff?" She is panicking because she wanted to meet them in the driveway before they got to the house. She doesn't want anything to mess up her parents' reunion.

*****

As Julian walks down the hallway to his bedroom, he has so many great feelings which helps put him at ease a little more about his decision to return to his family. He approaches the door and is suddenly confused. He doesn't know if he should knock or just walk directly into the room. He decides to give Christine some respect, so he knocks. While he's knocking, he thinks he hears another voice calling Christine's name, so he knocks again and patiently waits, but there is no answer.

He knocks again and calls out her name with a smile on his face. "Christine, it's me. Julian, your husband." He patiently waits for Christine to open the door, but he is getting anxious, so he grabs the doorknob and begins to twist it. He suddenly stops as he is thinking to himself, "What if she rejects me? I have no plan for that. Forget it. My day cannot get any crazier than it has already been."

*****

"What are you doing in my yard?" Heavenly asks the Dirty Boys. Slim replies with a sinister grin. "We live here now, little girl, so go on back in the house and watch TV or something."

Heavenly replies, "No, you don't live here. My dad is the only man who lives with us."

Slim replies with a smirk. "You are the chocolate one we heard about. Your mom didn't tell you about new living arrangements?" Slim and his boys begin to walk past Heavenly, as she stands there looking lost and confused, because she knows this is not the truth.

*****

Julian slowly begins to turn the knob. His heart is racing because he does not know what Christine's reaction will be and how much hurt she will be willing to forgive. He finally decides to push the door open all the way. "What the hell is going on Christine? Who the fuck is this man in my bed?"

Christine barely answers because she is just awakening. Julian cannot believe what his eyes are seeing—Christine lying in the arms of another man. He becomes furious. His anger reaches its highest level. He quickly rushes to the other side of the bed and snatches Andrew up by his neck. Andrew is barely awake. Julian says to Andrew as he squeezes his neck, "I advise you to get the fuck out of here right now, or it's not about to be a good scene for you or this broad."

Christine rolls over and grabs the cover as she is pleading with Julian to release Andrew unharmed. "What are you doing here? Me and you are not together. Please let him go!"

Andrew is calm as he says to Julian, "Hey, you can have her. Let me put my clothes on. I will leave your house."

Julian grabs his throat tighter. "While you think it's a game, I should put one in you for getting her on the shit."

With a smirk on his face, Andrew says, "Checkmate. You are the one who left her and your family for the love of your life."

Julian becomes angrier and punches him over and over again, while Christine begs for him to stop. Julian is so focused on hurting Andrew that he does not hear anything or see anything but his fist meeting Andrew's face.

*****

Heavenly comes out of her trance and runs in front of Slim and his boys as she starts yelling, "Daddy."

She runs to the living room, out of breath and anxious, and she asks Mark and Lindsey, "Have ya'll seen Dad? Is he in the bathroom?"

Mark and Lindsey continue to watch TV and shake their head no. Heavenly then advises her siblings to go to their room and don't come out until she comes to get them.

Mark replies, "Why we got to go in the room? My show is on."

Heavenly replies angrily, "Get in that room now, Mark, and never question me. Now, go if you trust me."

Mark and Lindsey turn the TV off and hurry to the room. Heavenly quickly kisses their foreheads as she says, "I love you."

Heavenly then runs toward her parents' room, only to be stopped dead in her tracks. She sees her father punching the same dude she shot at, and her mother once again begging, pleading, and crying for this man's life. Heavenly doesn't know what to do. She is stuck from the vision of her incident with this same man.

Christine yells to Heavenly as she notices her standing in the doorway. "Call the police, baby. Your father is going to kill him."

Heavenly doesn't respond. She is confused because she doesn't know what to do. She won't call the police on her father and have him put jail, but he is beating the man very badly. Just as Heavenly has figured out what to do, she turns to go out the door and get the neighbor, her dad's friend.

Slim and his boys hear the commotion and rush to the room, nearly knocking Heavenly over as they run in different directions. Slim runs into the room and immediately swings at Julian with a powerful right hook, knocking him to the bed and causing Julian to release Andrew. The Dirty Boys quickly grab Andrew and Slim pulls out his pistol to control the situation. Andrew lays there, coughing and bloody, but hysterically laughing in between every cough. Christine is begging Slim to let Julian go, sincerely crying for his safety.

Slim informs Christine of her choices as he says with a smile, "You have done your job. Now you can get the fuck out of here before I kill your dumb ass, too, broad. Matter of fact, if you call the police, I will kill this lame ass dude in front of your kids, so I dare you to tell. You know how much pull I got in these streets. So, I advise you to go to your kids and be a good mother for once."

Slim then turns to Julian as he says, "So, she finally let you go. I knew I would catch you slipping sooner or later. Crazy thing is, I thought when I popped you the first time you would disappear. Instead you get delivered right to me again." Slim looks at Andrew and says, "Good job, Checkmate." Slim focuses back on Julian who is lying across the bed with his hands up and he says, "I have one question for you, and the answer you give will determine if you live or die. Did you ever love her?"

Julian looks at Slim, puzzled and confused, as he says, "Who are you talking about? Man, please don't do this in front of my family."

Slim gives Julian a cold, evil look and says, "Family matters to you now, but family always mattered to me." Slim is angered by Julian's response, so he holds up the gun and says to him, "That was not the answer to my question, dude. Did you ever really love her?"

Julian blindly responds, "No, I love my family, my wife, and my kids."

Christine runs and yells for the kids to get their shoe on as she goes in the bathroom to put on some clothes from the dirty clothes hamper. She is scared to go back in the bedroom because Slim may kill her, and where would her children go?

Lindsey asks Christine, "Where is Dad and Heavenly? What is going on, Mom?"

Christine says, "Please listen to me right now. Put on your shoes and hurry up. Trust me."

Lindsey knows something isn't right, but she is confused about what is going on, so she listens to her mother.

*****

At this moment, Slim knows he has to keep his promise. Julian's response angered him, and his heart is racing because he knows what he has to do. Slim looks Julian in his eyes as he says, "Well I know where your loyalty lies, and I know who my loyalty is with—my family."

Slim pulls the trigger and Julian's lifeless body drops on the bed as the smoke from the gunshot waves in the air in front of his face. Slim still has the gun pointed at Julian's lifeless body, as he is in the zone. Slim is standing there, very satisfied with his actions. He is stuck there, staring at Julian.

Andrew grabs Slim and tells him they have to go. He gets in front of Slim and says, as he slowly grabs the gun, "Checkmate, we have to go before the cops come."

Slim releases the gun to Andrew. With a tear in his eye, he says, "I have been waiting on this for a very long time, fam."

*****

Christine and the children hear a loud bang. They all pause in a shock. As they try to identify the sound, they become very concerned. She advises the children to stay where they are. Christine runs toward her bedroom and she sees Julian lying on the bed with his eyes wide open, but no movement or sound. She runs up to Julian, trying to see if he will get up. She's crying, begging for him to get up, but she does not realize Julian has passed away.

She gently picks Julian's head up as she is confessing her love for him. "Please get up. I love you baby. I forgive you. We can get through this. I need you here. Please fight for us, for your kids."

*****

Meanwhile, Heavenly has gone to the neighbors and called 911. She is running up to the house when she sees Slim, Andrew, and the other two dudes running out the house. She passes them and she notices the gun in Andrew's hand. Heavenly rushes inside toward her parents' room and she makes an abrupt stop as she gets close to the entrance of the bedroom doorway.

She can't believe her eyes. All she can do is run to her dad, screaming, "No! Wake up, Dad! Please. You can't leave me again. No, Dad."

As Heavenly and Christine are trying to bring Julian back to life by doing CPR, they can hear the police and paramedics enter the house. Before Heavenly leaves the room to show the paramedics where her dad is, she says to Christine, "You did this to him. Why? He just wanted his family back, Mom."

Christine doesn't hear Heavenly. She is still trying to do CPR, hoping he comes to. Heavenly runs to the front door to get some help and show them where her father is located. She guides them to the room. The paramedics enter the room and say to Christine, "Please step back so we can do our job, ma'am."

"Thank you," the EMT says to Christine as he waves to the officer to assist. "Come this way, ma'am. The officer may need statements from you and your daughter. Is there anyone else in the home?"

Christine replies through her cries, "Yes, my other children are in the other room."

The officer replies, "We will need to secure this scene, and we will take all of you to the station for questioning. Go to the children and stay put."

The officer goes back in the room to see what is going on with the victim. The paramedic announces to the officer, "We have a thirty-nine-year-old male, no pulse, unresponsive, with a gunshot to the face. We have determined it as a DOA, dead on arrival. You can call the examiner. Our job is done here. Looks like a possible homicide." The paramedic leaves the scene and the officers begin to put up the tape for a crime scene. The officer calls the homicide department and the examiner, and then they take Christine and the children to the station.

Christine and the children sit and await the interview. She explains to Lindsey and Mark what has happened to their father. They begin to cry profusely, as Heavenly sits there quiet and in a daze.

An officer comes in to explain the process to Christine and the children. They each have to be questioned separately. He also asks if there is anyone who can sit with the children while they are interviewed, because none of the children are eighteen years of age. Christine gives the officer her closest family member's information.

CHAPTER SEVEN

~ Infatuation ~

The officer comes and gets Christine to do her interview. "Hello, Mrs. Valone. Can I call you Christine?" he asks.

Christine replies, "Yes you can. Give me a minute to hug and kiss my children, and then I will follow you." She kisses Mark and Lindsey and hugs them tightly. She approaches Heavenly and attempts to hug her, but Heavenly pulls away from her and goes to the corner of the room. The officer gestures to her to hurry up the process. Sadly, she looks at Heavenly who has her back turned to her, and walks away.

"Hello, Mrs. Valone. I am a homicide detective. My name is Sam. I will be interviewing you today." He pulls out the chair, inviting Christine to have a seat. As she sits down, she has tears flowing down her face.

Sam offers her a Kleenex and says, "First, I want to say I am sorry for your loss. Thank you for speaking with me. I will be asking you a variety of questions and I will be writing

114

and recording everything you have said to me." He informs her he is about to start the interview and turns on the recorder. "Do you know who did this to your husband?"

Christine looks at the detective and says as she crying, "Yes, I did that to my husband." Christine breaks down and confesses her role in Julian's murder.

The detective informs Christine as he says, "I know you are upset, but this is final. I am not saying that you are wrong, but you must know we will use this in court."

Christine replies, "I must tell the truth. That is all that matters now. I should have never invited them to my house, but my habit got the best of me," Christine says.

Sam replies, "Who are you are referring to?"

Christine replies, "Slim, Andrew, and the Dirty Boys; they killed Julian."

Sam continues to write notes in regards to what Christine has disclosed to him. Sam asks, "Do you know any of their real names, or have they ever been arrested?"

Christine replies, "I know Andrew's last name, which is Smith. Slim has been in jail before, upstate to be specific."

Christine's eyes are constantly full of tears and Sam feels sympathy for her as he states, "We can take a break if you really need to. I know this is overwhelming, so just stop me if it becomes too much. I can get you some water, coffee, or tea."

Christine looks at the detective through her blurry eyes and says, "No, thank you. How could I be so careless? I knew Andrew was secretly jealous of Julian. That's why I said I killed him."

Sam asks permission to walk to the other side of the table to comfort Christine. He rubs her back and passes her some more Kleenex. "Did you see Andrew, Slim, or anyone else pull the trigger?" he asks.

Christine pauses for a second, then says, "No, I didn't see anything. I heard a loud bang and I told the kids to stay in the room. I ran to my bedroom where I saw Julian lying on the bed, dying. Slim, Andrew, and the other two dudes ran past me going out the door. Look at me. I have his blood everywhere." Christine grabs some of the Kleenex and tries to wipe off some of the dried blood.

Sam notices Christine needs a break as he watches her wiping dried blood with a dry Kleenex. He lets her know he is leaving the room to give her moment to pull herself together. He leaves and starts to look for a female detective to arrest Christine.

Sam sees detective Jean at her desk. He explains what has happened and asks for her assistance. She agrees and then says, "So is that the wife?"

Sam replies, "Yes, it is legally his wife. Same last names too."

Jean looks in the interview room to see what she looks like, then says, "Sure is his wife. I was working on another case involving these same parties. Funny thing is, I predicated this before it even happened."

Just as they were discussing the details of Christine's confession, they both turn around to see what all the commotion is about at the front desk. They both notice a woman who sounds like she is really upset.

The woman says to the officer at the desk, "Sir, I am looking for my boyfriend. His name is Julian Valone. Someone said he is here, so where is he?"

The officer replies, "Ma'am, you will need to stay calm so I can check my system. Can you please take a seat? When I find out where he is, I will let you know. Thank you."

As she nervously takes a seat, she looks around the room to get her mind off being in the station and notices Julian's name on the board. She gets up and heads toward the desk as she says, "He is here. I see his name on the board over there. I need to see him right now."

The officer looks at the board and notices that his name is indeed there. The woman doesn't know that the board is for unsolved homicides that are being worked on. He does not want to alarm the woman because she is already upset. He looks in the system to see which detective is working on the case and says, "Ma'am, I will have a detective come speak with you shortly."

The officer calls up the lead detective on the case. "Jean, I need you at the front desk. I have a woman here looking for Julian Valone and she is upset."

Jean replies, "I am on my way. I am actually right down the hall and I did hear how upset she is."

Jean explains to Sam there is another person involved in this case and she is at the desk. She will return to book Christine. Jean heads down the hall to the desk to help the woman and see what she may know about the case.

The officer at the desk introduces Jean as she walks up. "Jean, this woman is looking for her boyfriend, Julian Valone."

Jean replies, "Thank you, Officer. I will take it from here. Come this way with me, ma'am."

They begin to walk to Jean's desk. She needs to question her as well as give her the bad news. She says, "Please have a seat. May I ask what your name is? Please forgive me for being so rude."

The woman replies, "My name is Charlene Smith and I just want to see Julian."

Jean looks up her name in the computer and realizes she is the girlfriend from the hospital. As Jean hears the woman's name again, it sounds familiar. She looks familiar, but she doesn't know why. She has a puzzled look on her face. Jean looks at Charlene and tries to figure out a way to break the news easily, because she doesn't think Charlene is aware of Julian's death

"First of all, I must give my condolences to you for your loss," Jean says.

Charlene looks confused as if she has not yet comprehended the words Jean has told her. She says, "What the hell you mean 'my loss,' lady. Who had a loss? Not me."

Jean replies as she gives a long sigh, "Julian is no longer with us. He was murdered today. Again, I am sorry for your loss."

Charlene drops to the floor and instantly starts to cry as she yells, "Ya'll always lying to folks. Ya'll done killed him before he could make it here, and now ya'll blaming it on someone else. Talking about some damn homicide. Hell no."

Jean goes to the other side of her desk to comfort Charlene, who is on her knees crying and yelling uncontrollably. Charlene cannot wrap her mind around what she has just been told. She doesn't want it to be true, after what had just happened with her and Julian hours ago. She never told him the real truth about her feelings.

*****

The children sit the waiting area, holding each other tightly and crying, but none of them utters a word.

"Hello, Heavenly, Mark, and Lindsey. I am Bonnie, the social worker. I would like to speak with the three of you about what happened today, but we are waiting for your aunt Theresa. All of you are under eighteen, so we must have a parent or guardian here for the interview. I know what happened to your father was horrible, and we would like to catch the bad guy who did this to him." Bonnie notices that Heavenly is covered in dried blood. "Heavenly, would you like to get some clean clothes?"

Heavenly stares at Bonnie angrily and says, "The bad guy is our mother, and I am fine. This is all I have left of him—his blood, inside and out."

Bonnie knows that the children have been through a lot, so she takes that into consideration. "Are you children hungry?" she asks.

Mark and Lindsey look to Heavenly for permission to answer, but Heavenly replies, "Feed those two. I will be okay, so thank you anyways."

Bonnie gets up and walks out of the room to get the children some food and maybe a stuffed animal to comfort them. As Bonnie exits the room and closes the door, she says to her colleague, "They really look up to the older sibling, Heavenly, and she always answers for them as they look to her for permission. So we need to be careful when we ask questions, because they may shut down if she doesn't give them permission."

After they are left alone, Heavenly tells Mark and Lindsey about the social worker. "Do not tell these people anything about our life," she says. "They will use our words to make us mad at each other. We will always stick together as a family. Pinky promise." They move to unite their pinky fingers.

"Heavenly, what happened to Daddy?" Mark asks.

Heavenly replies, "I don't know and neither do either of you." She pulls Mark and Lindsey closer to her as she holds them and kisses their foreheads.

*****

Sam enters the interview room, passes her a cup of water, and says, "Mrs. Valone, I hope you are feeling calmer now."

Christine gives him her attention as she sips the water and nods her head yes.

"I must be honest with you. We found an ounce of cocaine in the light fixture in your kitchen ceiling. Would you like to tell me how it got there?" Sam asks.

Christine looks at Sam in disbelief. Speechless, she pauses before she says, "I don't know what you are talking about."

Sam replies, "Well it got there somehow, and aren't you and your husband the homeowners?"

"Yes, we are, but I don't know how that got there. We didn't put it there," Christine says.

"If you or your husband did not put it there, maybe it was your boyfriend or Slim the drug dealer, both of whom you invited to your home. Or was it there for your personal use?" Sam asks.

Christine replies, "I told you I don't know what you're talking about. I stand by my statement."

Sam looks Christine directly in her eyes and firmly says, "Is there a $100,000 life insurance policy on your husband?"

Christine becomes agitated as she says, "Oh, my God. You can't be serious! I've had that policy for four years now. I just lost my husband and possibly my children. How could you be so cruel?"

Sam replies, "I heard you were having financial troubles. You have a new boyfriend and your husband left you with three children to take care of. Sounds like a great motive to me."

Christine is crying profusely and shaking her head no, as if that was the answer to the detective's question.

Sam says to Christine, "Well, I see this interview is over. You are lying about something and I am not sure what it is, but could you stand up for me?" At that very moment, Jean comes in as he is arresting Christine. He says, "You are under arrest for the murder of Julian Valone, drug possession, and neglect."

Christine is trembling and crying as she says, "Why would I kill someone I truly loved all my life?"

Sam replies, "A lot of people have their own motives. Maybe you do too. She's all yours, Jean."

Christine turns around so that Jean can handcuff her and take her to booking. Jean informs Sam that she still has Charlene at her desk as she begins to take Christine to booking. Christine is still pleading her innocence as she is walking down the hall, repeatedly saying, "I did not kill Julian. He was my husband."

Charlene looks up when she thinks she hears Julian's name. She stops crying to focus more on what she thinks she just heard. Charlene gets up to follow the commotion and she realizes it's Christine in handcuffs yelling, "I did not kill my husband. I loved him all my life."

Charlene instantly becomes angry as she hears the words Christine is yelling. She runs closer to where Christine and the detectives are standing, still in disbelief of her pleas. Charlene is so angry that, without noticing it, words just come out her mouth. "You lowlife broad, you killed my man because he left you for me."

The detective pushes Charlene back and guides her back to Jean's desk as she uncontrollably cries.

Christine yells down the hall, "He didn't want you. He wanted me and his family," as she drops her head.

*****

Meanwhile, at the other end of the station, the social worker sits in the interview area as she watches the children eat their food. She suddenly turns her attention to the door because she hears a few knocks. She excuses herself from the children to address the unexplained knocks at the door.

It is another social worker who occupies the other side of the door. She says, "Bonnie, the children's aunt Theresa is in the waiting area, asking to speak with you."

Bonnie exits the room to go speak with the children's aunt. Bonnie walks up to Theresa and introduces herself. "Hello, Theresa. I am Bonnie, the social worker with the New Orleans Police Department. I don't know if you are aware of what has happened, but let me inform you now. There was an incident in your sister's home in which someone lost their life. That someone would be Julian, her husband. The children were also there. I am not sure if they saw anything, but they are aware that Julian has passed. Here's the reason why you were called: the children can either go to a foster home, or they can go with you, the next of kin. I am not sure what your lifestyle is like, or how your relationship is with the children, but we are giving you the option of taking them home."

Theresa has no response and not many emotions to the news of Julian's death. She never cared for Julian because of the way he treated Christine. Theresa replies, "Where is my sister? Is she okay? And the children?"

"Your sister is fine, but she has been arrested for murder, drug possession, and neglect," Bonnie says.

"You all are some damn fools to think my sister killed Julian or had anything to do with his death," Theresa says. "She loved that man more than she loved her own flesh and blood. Overall, I know my sister is innocent and I will take my nieces and nephew with me. They have been through enough." Theresa shakes her head in disbelief at what the social worker had stated.

Bonnie replies, "Theresa, there is a process to keep them in your home. They can go with you tonight if they are willing to go, but I will be by tomorrow to start the process.

We still have not interviewed the children, but when we are done, you're free to take them home."

"Would you like to see them now?" Bonnie asks Theresa.

Theresa replies sarcastically, "Yes, I would like to see them. I know they are scared to death, all of you strangers around asking questions." Theresa follows Bonnie out the door, down the hall to where the children are eating and awaiting her return.

She opens the door and lets Theresa walk in first, so she can see the children's reactions when they see their aunt. Lindsey and Mark are very excited to see Theresa. They run directly to her. But Heavenly, on the other hand, is very vague and uninterested in her presence.

As Bonnie sits down, she notes the reaction the children had and notices Heavenly looking uneasy. Bonnie approaches Theresa and informs her that she will take Mark first. She says, "I will take Mark with me first so I can speak with just him, but you have to be present, Theresa." Bonnie notices Mark is looking for approval from Heavenly before he moves. She nods her head for him to follow Bonnie.

Mark and Theresa follow Bonnie down the hall to start the interview. As they are about to enter the interview room, Mark suddenly throws a tantrum and says, "No, take me back to my sisters. I want Heavenly here with me." Bonnie and Theresa instantly turn around to soothe Mark. Mark calms down and looks at Bonnie, grabs her hand, and says, "When my dad died, it sounded like a big door closing really hard. I am scared."

Bonnie slowly guides Mark to the table and has him take a seat as she pulls a chair directly in front of him. Bonnie asks Mark, "Do you mind if your aunt Theresa comes in here with us?"

Mark replies, "Yes she can come in. I won't be scared then because both of you can protect me.

Bonnie replies, "Okay, Mark. Can I go in the hallway and get her? I will come right back and I will leave the door open so you can see both of us coming in.

He looks up at Bonnie with very sad eyes and tries to be brave as he says, "I will be okay, just leave the door open, please."

Bonnie walks toward the door to get Theresa from the hallway and she leaves it open so Mark can see the both of them. Theresa enters the room with Bonnie. Mark brightens up a little as if they were his heroes. Bonnie says to Mark, "Now that your aunt is here, do you feel more comfortable talking to me?"

Mark replies with a smile on his face as he says, "Yes, Ma'am."

Bonnie pulls out her pen and pad as she begins to ask Mark some questions. "Do you remember anything about what happened today? If you don't want to answer we can just go on to the next questions."

Mark replies, "No Ma'am, I don't know anything. My mom told me and Lindsey to stay in the room until she comes back."

Bonnie says, "So, you said earlier that you heard a sound that scared you. Since you didn't see anything, was the sound close or far away? Or anything else that you would like for me to know?"

"The sound was close, and I don't have anything else to tell you," Mark replies

Bonnie asks, "Can you tell me anything about your dad or your family?"

"No Ma'am."

Bonnie says, "Well, Theresa, it looks like he doesn't have much to say, so I will interview the other children now. You can take Mark down the hall and bring Lindsey back with you. Thank you, Mark. You did very well." Mark looks at Bonnie with a smile on his face as he turns and walks out the door with Theresa.

Theresa now walks back with Lindsey to the interview room. Bonnie stands as she greets Lindsey and guides her to the seat Mark was sitting in. She says, "Hello, Lindsey."

Lindsey replies, "Hi, Lady." Lindsey is different from Mark. She is smiling and definitely very warm to Bonnie's presence.

Bonnie gives Lindsey a very big, bright, warm smile in return as she says, "I am going to ask you a few questions about what happened today. You don't have to answer the questions if you do not want to. Do you remember anything about today? Any sounds or noise, Lindsey?" She wanted to address her by her name so the conversation would sound more personal and friendly.

Lindsey replies, "I remember fighting, yelling, a big bang noise—it kind of sounded like heavy doors closing—and I heard Heavenly screaming."

Bonnie listens to Lindsey as she writes down everything she says. She also observes her emotions which differ from her brother's. Bonnie replies, "Wow, that seems like a lot of things going on at one time. I know you and your brother were scared and confused from all the noise."

Lindsey replies, "I hear different noises all the time, but it scared me to hear Heavenly crying and screaming. She never cries."

Bonnie asks, "Does Heavenly always stay strong and protect you?"

Lindsey replies, "Yes, she knows everything like God. She takes care of me and my brother."

"So, would it be safe to say Heavenly is like a mother to the both of you, or is she more of a sister?" Bonnie asks.

Lindsey replies, "Well, she is my sister, but she kind of acts like a mother. She cooks, cleans, and taught me how to use the washer after I wet the bed. She helps us with homework and she puts us to bed every day.

Bonnie says, "Well, Heavenly seems like a great big sister. I wish I had a sister like her. Me and my sister used to fight all the time, but we really loved each other. Sort of like you and your siblings, except my sister was not as great as Heavenly."

"Yes, she is great, unless we don't listen to her; then she will yell really loud at us. Please don't tell her anything I told you," Lindsey says.

"I promise I won't say anything, but when she is upset, does she hit you?" Bonnie asks.

Lindsey replies, "No, silly Milly. She would never do that; she just won't give us snacks."

Bonnie replies, "Thank you, I really appreciate you sharing that information with me, Lindsey. You are a great little girl and please stay sweet." She smiles and gestures that they are free to go, and then she tells Theresa that she can bring Heavenly to the room.

Theresa exits with Lindsey. Lindsey turns around to go back and hug Bonnie. Bonnie's hearts melts for the little girl who just wants adults to be nice to her. Bonnie has come to the conclusion, as Lindsey had put so much emphasis on what Heavenly does, that adults either haven't paid much attention to her, or they have been very mean to her.

Heavenly walks slowly behind Theresa as if she doesn't want to be seen with her. Heavenly stops and says to her aunt, "Why are you here like you care?"

Theresa replies, "Excuse me, did you say something to me, little girl?"

Heavenly ignores Theresa and rolls her eyes. As they enter the room, Heavenly's emotional state changes instantly.

Bonnie says, "Hello, beautiful young lady, do you want to have a seat?"

Heavenly replies, "Listen, Bonnie, I am fine standing here. Just ask whatever and let us go home, Lady."

Bonnie knows she has to take a very strategic approach with Heavenly. She is protective and has her guard up against anyone who invades her privacy. Bonnie notices her body language—hands in her pockets, eyes directly on her as she stands stern and very still. This shows a sign of control and plenty of self-control.

Bonnie says to Heavenly, "I notice that you are a very intelligent young lady. I think it's cool to be smart and pretty in today's world. I know what happened today must be hard to deal with—the loss of both parents, you're away from home, and you have to go to your aunt's house. Those are a lot of events to happen in one day. Clearly, I understand that this all occurred because your father was looking for you, but. . ."

Bonnie is unable to finfish her sentence because she is rudely interrupted by Heavenly who says, "First of all, it was my mother's fault and that snake boyfriend of hers. I would never get my father killed or even harmed, for that matter. I love my father and he was my everything. That whorish mother of mine is who killed him. He only came back to get his family back and start our lives over. I am done. This is stupid. You know what the hell happened." Heavenly storms out of the room and down the hall to where her siblings are waiting.

Bonnie looks at Theresa who seems very upset. "I never meant to upset her, Mrs. Theresa. I just wanted information on the murder."

Theresa replies, "You definitely got the information you needed about my sister. I will be down the hall with the children if you need me."

Bonnie finishes writing her notes and heads down to the waiting area where the family is located. As Bonnie walks into the room, everyone watches her movements. She says, "Well, Mrs. Theresa Newman, here is the documentation for the children to be released to you. Sign where the Xs are and you will be free to go home."

Theresa signs the papers and gathers the children to leave the precinct.

Bonnie says to Theresa, "I will be in touch with you in the next 72 hours so I can check the children's living arrangements. Here is my card if you have any questions before I contact you. Have a good night, guys. See you soon."

Bonnie watches Theresa and the children leave. A feeling of sadness comes over her because she has a soft spot for troubled children. She knows from past experience these children will be damaged, but to what extent is the question.

CHAPTER EIGHT
~ The Rebirth of a Goddess ~

"We have picked up Andrew Smith and Shawn Smith. Andrew is in interview room one and Shawn is in room two."

Jean replies to Simon, "You can interview Andrew, but I want to interview Shawn. There's something about him that doesn't sit right with me. I will take interview room two with Steve as my partner. I advise you to take Tony. He will be your balance, hot head."

She goes to get Steve so they can do the interview. Jean says to him, "Let me do the talking, Steve. He may not give us any information if you lead the interview. He seems to be intimidated by a male presence." They both walk into the interview room and introduce themselves and explain why they are questioning his involvement.

"Hello, Mr. Smith, my name is detective Jean from homicide and this is detective Steve. You are here because someone pointed you out as the monster that killed an unarmed man." She extends her hand to him.

Mr. Smith replies, "Listen, lady. I don't shake hands with people unless we are doing business with you."

Jean replies, "Okay, so let's get down to the business then, Slim. You were named as the killer. I will be asking questions and you can answer or choose not to. This conversation will be recorded and my partner will be documenting it as well." She looks Slim directly in the eyes as she turns on the recorder and says, "Why did you kill Julian?"

Slim sits straight up in his chair and stares at Jean with an evil, sinister smile. Jean has never come across this type of reaction, so she watches his every move. He asks, "Do you smoke, sexy lady?"

Jean replies, "No, I don't."

Slim replies, "Does this tequila drinking motherfucker have one?"

Steve never says a sword. He passes Jean the pack of cigarettes without taking his eyes off Slim. Due to his comment, he doesn't care for Slim's sarcasm.

Jean passes Slim the ashtray and the pack of cigarettes with a book of matches. After he lights the cigarette, she extends her hand out for the matches to be returned.

Slim smiles. "I know this Creole smokes. Can't have tequila without a nice smoke." Slim looks at both of the detectives and says, "What I am about to tell you is going down in history. Let me know when you are ready, because I have been waiting to be able to tell this story for a long time.

Jean smiles at Slim and sarcastically says, "Well, since I noticed you like to take control, whenever you are ready, I will be your personal audience, sitting here waiting to listen to your history-making story.

Slim sits straight up and looks at the detectives with his hands are crossed. He pulls a drag off the cigarette, then he begins to tell his story. "Well, when I was younger, my father died which made me head of the household. My mom would always tell me to get myself together and help take care of the family. My mom didn't have much education, but she always had a job. She was very hard worker. I would see my aunts and uncles helping her as best they could, but it was still not enough. I would see their frustration as they had to constantly help my mother. All the family was really close, so no one ever said anything, but as a kid you watch everything adults do. At that point, I knew when I got older I needed to help her out. I only had one option—go to school, get a job, and graduate. At sixteen, I started working. I wasn't making much money, but I thought it helped. That was still not enough to take the hardship off my mother. So, I figured I would go get another job and worked those two jobs for about three years. While my mom had some relief, I had become angry and frustrated. I started trying to figure out how to make some quick money and start living life. I was young and never even enjoyed one check because I felt guilty for all the years my mother had to struggle, so I would keep very little for myself. I started talking to a few kids from around the way that was doing their thing, and they easily convinced me to become my own boss. You know what I mean."

Slim smiles really wide while he explains this part of the story—the happier times in his life. "My homeboy who was well known for getting paper, connected me to his connect, and I was on ever since then. You feel me? My family didn't know I was hustling, so I kept my business running during the hours I was supposed to be at work. My mom and sister never knew what I was doing for a very long time. I was able to keep it a secret because my mom only went to work and came home.

My little sister only went to school and family members' houses."

"My mom found out years later from my uncle. He came to my little spot and copped some work. He recognized my voice. I didn't show my face when I served them, so when I asked what he wanted, he called me by my first name, not my street name. So, I came out and begged him to keep it to himself. He agreed to keep quiet, but when I stopped giving him credit for the work, he got angry and he told my mom. My mom called me. She was devastated, yelling and calling me the devil. It was cool, but she kicked me out of the house and didn't want me around my sister. It was bad for my family. I had to sneak around just to see my little sister for a few seconds. We were very close and it hurt me to leave my sister. She needed a male figure in her life. I would go to the school, sign her out early just so I could spend a day with her. My sister was torn as well. Every night we would talk on the phone before she went to bed, but one thing we always did was pray before we hung up. I told her I would one day make enough money and start a legit business that she could run, so she definitely needed to graduate and go to college. We had a partnership. She was going to be a financial advisor. I always took care of my family, myself, and my workers too."

"At this time, I am feeling good about life. My baby sister is about to graduate and go to college. Life is awesome right now. You know what I'm saying? Unfortunately, a few things start going wrong, especially with my sister. I hear about this guy who is trying to talk to my sister and I hear she really like this dude. So, I ask her about this dude. Of course, she lies at first, but I found out who the little dude is. I press the little dude, and told him who I was and if he didn't leave her alone I was going to kill him if he goes near her again. I really thought I got through to the little dude because my name ring bells in the street. I say what I mean, nothing less. I also warned my sister, if I catch him with her I will hurt his little ass. She ignored me too. I guess she thought she was in love or some shit, but I told her how these dudes be doing females because I am one of them dudes. For real, though, she knows how I hurt a lot of chicks, and I personally didn't care to know how or when they were hurt. I was having fun doing me. Honestly, I kept it real from the beginning so the chicks were down with. I wanted sex when I was ready, with no emotions involved. I was chasing money but there was no loyalty."

Slim pauses for a while. He seems to be in a complete daze as he carries on to say, "So, anyways, my little sister did go on to graduate and I throw a nice party. All my family came except for my mother. I really hoped that she would show up because it was my sister, and I missed my mother. I was hoping this was a time she could forgive me and, as a family, move forward. I even thought about what I would say to her if she did show up, but that went down the drain when I realized she was not coming."

Slim continues to tell his story with tears in his eyes as he says, "I knew right then she had written me off as her son for good. After realizing that my mother didn't care, I didn't care about nothing and no one but my little sister from that point on. I really loved my mom. I was lost, but shit, I am a grown ass man so I didn't sweat it. As all this was transpiring between me and my mom, we forgot who hurt the most—my little sister was caught in the middle and she loved both of us. She never took any sides because she understood both of us. In the process, she became very lost and leaned more to the streets. This little dude to be specific. I didn't realize how serious it had become until she told me she was not going to college. I tried to talk her out of it, but she was not listening at all, so I had to find this dude again. So, I find the little dude and question him about my sister's decision. He denies it as I thought he would. This dude tries to tell me they are just friends, like I'm stupid. I knew exactly what that meant. She was not the only chick he was dealing with at that time. I'm like, this little dude a player and my sister is definitely in trouble. And he's like, you can't believe that my type really loves you. That was really making me angry because he was lying, so I warned him for the last time and I meant everything I told him."

Slim blankly stares at the wall as he talks about his sister and this little dude, as if the little dude was in the room and he was talking to him at that moment. Jean looks at Slim, whom seems to be off track, so she focuses his attention back to the story by asking, "What did you say to him, Slim?"

Slim replies, "I told that motherfucker I would kill him if he hurts my sister. I held the glock to his head, then I killed the silly dude."

Jean and Steve look at each other as she says, "So Slim, are you confessing to the murder of Julian Valone?"

Slim replies, "Yes I am. I have no regrets and you got what you want, so go ahead and lock me up."

Jean replies, "May I ask you why you are not remorseful?"

Slim gives Jean a serious, emotionless stare as he says, "I told this dude to stop playing with me, but he did the ultimate bullshit which sent me over the edge. I was at my spot when I got the call, one of the worst calls a brother can receive. My mom, who hated the sound of my voice or the sight of me, called me crying. She must have dropped the phone because I can hear her in the background stating how Charlene went to the emergency room for attempting suicide and she was not responsive when they took her from the house. I instantly jumped in my car to meet them at the hospital, but I was speeding all the way there. I wasn't stopping until I got to my sister. She needed me. All I was thinking was if she dies without saying goodbye to me, I couldn't live with that. She was my everything. I knew that Julian was the cause of her doing this, but if my sister died or even if she didn't, he was going die for putting her through all this shit. I just wanted to tell her I love her and I'm here for her always."

"I never really focused on my speed, so the police tried to pull me over. I took them on a high-speed chase to the hospital. I was told I crashed just before I reached the hospital and was unconscious. I woke up a few days later with officers at my door, and I instantly started asking about my sister. The officer said he would have the nurse check on the person I was referring to because I was in custody, so I couldn't leave the room. I was so devastated, I started crying and yelling. The nurse came in and informed me how Charlene was doing, but she mentioned a baby. I told her she did not have the right person. My sister was not pregnant; she tried to commit suicide. Apparently, she was pregnant, and when I pressed Julian, he broke it off with Charlene and was with another chick named Christine and was really in love with her. I didn't realize how much she loved this dude, but he broke my sister's spirit, not just her heart, and that cannot be easily fixed. I know from experience."

Jean starts to sympathize with Slim and she says, "I knew her name started to sound familiar. I was one of the detectives on the scene and it was heart wrenching to see a young woman wanting to take her life over something she cannot control."

Slim replies, "So, now that you got your answer about my remorse, you can just take me to jail, because I been waiting for twelve years to find him and destroy his family as he did with mine. So, remorse? Hell naw, I don't feel no damn remorse.

Jean replies, "So what parts do Andrew and Christine play in this situation?"

Slim replies to Jean question. "Technically, I used Andrew to get Christine, and she went for it. Christine was a dumb broad looking for some attention because my sister had her husband, so I sent my cousin to give her some attention. I realized she was in a vulnerable state and he was thirsty looking for love, so I used both of them to get close to Julian. Yeah, I already know. I am a fucking genius."

Jean looks at Slim with disgust because he's proud of taking someone's life. She says, "Steve will take you to booking, as you have confessed your part and I need to do paperwork. Before you go, do you know you made it worse? Charlene doesn't have you or Julian. Who's going to keep her out of the psychiatric ward now? But I guess you didn't think of that, genius."

Slim holds his head down as if he is ashamed of his actions now.

As Jean walks back to her desk to do the report, all she can think of is how Charlene will react to all of this mess. The scene of Charlene's suicide attempt is stuck in her head. She never would have suspected that they were siblings or that Andrew was related to them as their cousin. A great sadness overcomes Jean as she realizes that Charlene and Christine were both victims from the beginning. Jean sits at her desk as she looks at picture of the bloody scene from Julian's murder.

*****

Meanwhile, Andrew is being interviewed by detectives Simon and Tony. Simon leads the interview as he says, "We already know that you and Shawn killed Julian, so what else can you tell me, like what was your role in this crime?"

Andrew replies, "Yo, I didn't kill no one. That was Christine and Slim who plotted to kill Julian. Shit, they used me to be a part if their game. I found out a lot of shit. Neither one of them are who they say they are. Slim had been messing with Christine before I was, and this went on for a while. They really thought no one knew, but I knew it all. They used to meet twice a week at the hotel, around midnight every time. I only knew this because one night I came to the hotel to cop some work and she was there. I really didn't know who she was, but I knew she was bad. I stared at her because she was just naturally beautiful with a beautiful body to go with it. I told him he was lucky. If I had someone like that in my bed, I wouldn't answer the door or the phone. I would be in it all night long. I actually was trying to get a piece that night. I was high and I was feeling her, wishing she was in my bed. Slim noticed the way I was staring at her and asked did I want her. Of course, I said hell yea. He said that was one of his main chicks. He will hook me up later. I couldn't stop thinking about her, so I continuously asked him about hooking me up. I had broken up with my girl about year prior to seeing Christine. I needed a real woman to be with me on a regular basis."

"Slim told me about this woman he knew around the way. She was going through some things, but she was a good woman. I asked him how he knew the woman, because he only mess with loose women. He explained she lived in the neighborhood and she came and copped from him once in a while, but she was not his type. I asked him to speak with her and make it happen one day soon. A couple of weeks later, he called me over to the spot to meet with her. When I arrived, she was sitting in the house laughing and drinking with Slim. I didn't know why, but she looked so familiar to me. She was just naturally beautiful. She had long, natural hair, caramel smooth skin, everything was covered up and she didn't have on no make-up. I was in love with her from the very first time I saw her. So, I started having a conversation with her and then I got the courage to ask her out on a date. To my surprise, she instantly said yes. I am feeling like the man, because I never had this type of woman even pay attention to me. We went on a few dates, and we were feeling each other real hard. I didn't catch any feelings for her until after we had sex, but I loved her natural beauty. She was awesome. She fulfilled my need for a companion and sex. I filled her need for love and compassion."

"After a while, it became serious and we wanted to see each other more, but she had children whom I didn't know yet. I wasn't ready to be daddy, but I definitely wanted all of her attention. She was not comfortable with me coming to her house because of her children, so we would always be at my apartment. Slim saw how close we were getting and questioned me about expanding his business around the area. I thought it was a bad idea at first because of her children, but when he said we would receive all work for free, he was talking my lingo. So, I ran it across Christine one time and she was so concerned about what her husband would think about the whole thing, it made me angry. He left her and the kids, but she worried about his feelings. It just didn't make any sense to me. After all, I continued to remind her how expensive our habit was, so she eventually agreed to think about it. We had been dating for over a year now and I decided to ask can I come over. We had a long night of partying and having fun, so we went to her house which was closer, because we were both wasted. When I woke up the next morning, all I saw was her beautiful face. The best feeling in the world. She cooked breakfast, we had sex, and I went home feeling like the man."

"I stayed over at least twice a week after that, but I never saw her children. I only heard them as they were getting ready for school. One day, I stayed over after we had a great night. We were so wasted, we decided to go to her house because it was closer. We woke up and, as normal, we do our thing. I was not aware of any of the children being home, but that oldest girl was home. That little motherfucker tried to kill me with somebody's gun. She had a silver 9mm pointed at me, and this bitch really pulled the trigger, but it didn't hit me. It went past me and into the wall. Man, I thought I was gone because I heard the bullet when it passed by my ear. I never seen a little girl handle a gun like that. Shit was crazy. She was screaming something about her dad, so I assumed Christine had not told them about me yet. So, I told Christine to tell her who I was and she ignored me. All I know is that I wanted to get the fuck out of there."

Simon looks at Andrew in disbelief as he says, "So you are telling me a seventeen-year-old girl shot at you with a 9mm?"

Andrew replies, "I cannot make this shit up. Man, this little girl was mad as hell. Anyways, as I was saying, that same day her father came looking for her. Apparently, after the incident, she left the house upset and no one knew where she was. As he is looking for the little girl, he somehow tumbles over to Slim's spot. They beat him and shot him, but he didn't die as they intended for him to. So that's when Slim called me and said the woman I mess with, her husband tried to rob him and he think he killed the man. I was confused about the whole situation because that man is not built like that, to rob one of the biggest dealers in the area. So I called Christine. She did verify he had been beaten and shot, but he was not dead. I gave her my sympathy and hung up the phone. I called Slim back and told him that dude was nothing to worry about. He was not dead and he is at the hospital. Slim replies, 'We got to kill this dude before he tries to kill my fam.' I totally agreed with him because at that time, I wasn't aware of any connection with him and Christine, but I definitely wasn't going to see my family get hurt. These streets are cold. At that very moment, we had to do something, so we came up with a plan to just find him and torture him, but not kill him. He clearly had tried to rob the wrong person, and you don't let shit like that slide. At this point, I am not aware that Slim is telling lies about the robbery, so I do my part. I talked to Christine again about setting up shop at her house and she finally agrees to let my cousin use her house. She just wanted it shut down by a certain time because of the kids."

"The day we came to set up the camera and everything else, Slim sends Christine to the store to get some liquor. I went in her room to see if I could get a quick fix, because she always kept it in her dresser drawer. There was nothing in there, so I started searching around the room in other drawers. As I was looking for the work, I stumble across an identification card. It looks a lot like Christine, but the name says Angie Ruiz with a different address. This was awkward, and I am trying to figure out why she would have a fake identification card. As I was sitting on the bed in my thoughts, I heard Slim call me to come play the game with him."

Tony looks confused as he says to Andrew, "So are you saying Christine has two identities?"

Andrew replies, "Hell yeah, that's exactly what I am saying. Shit shocked me too. When I questioned her about it, she got really upset and said, 'That is my friend who passed away,' and I was being disrespectful for going through her things. I apologized and went on with my day, but I couldn't let it go that easy. I thought back to when Slim told me some girl named Angie he didn't know came to see him and she offered him a business position, but he turned her down."

Simon smiles as he says to Andrew, "So, Christine and Angie is the same person, and somehow she was plotting with Slim?"

Andrew replies, "I don't give a damn who believes me. I know I didn't kill nobody. Check Slim's visitation records and you will see that I am not lying. I should be getting less time or some money for the shit I just told you, dumb motherfuckers."

Simon chuckles as he is trying understand Andrew's story. "So, Andrew, is this a confession of your involvement, or a mere statement of your side of the story?"

Andrew smirks as he looks at the two sitting across from him and replies, "Call it what you want. I just told what I know."

Tony asks Andrew to stand up and says, "You are under arrest for the murder of Julian Valone. I will be taking you to booking."

Tony leaves the room to do the paperwork for the case, but he feels that Andrew may be telling the truth in some parts of his story. Tony says to Simon as he walks in the opposite direction, "Make sure he is not on the same floor as his cousin. I am going to find Jean. She has to read this paperwork. There is something not right with case."

Simon replies, "We just got a full-blown confession from this guy; all the rest is irrelevant."

They both go in different directions. Tony finds Jean and tells her what Andrew confessed as they compare notes.

Jean looks at Tony and says, "Did Andrew ask for representation?"

Tony replies, "No, he didn't and that is unusual for his type."

Jean replies, "We just got a full-blown confession from Slim as well, but what puzzles me is he never asked for representation. He has money and he just voluntarily confessed."

Jean sits at her desk, going through the papers, trying to figure out what exactly is the truth in this case.

CHAPTER NINE

~ Addiction to the Light ~

Theresa arrives home with the children and begins to help them settle in. Mark and Lindsey look around in disbelief at how beautiful her house is. The children have not visited their aunt for many years.

Theresa walks around and shows them where they will be sleeping as she says, "So, I have a guest room for Mark to sleep in. Heavenly and Lindsey, you two can sleep in my family room. There is a pull-out bed in the couch."

Heavenly rolls her eyes and says, "Put me and Lindsey in the family room like throwaways, I guess."

Theresa replies, "I guess you act just like your dirty dick ass father. I am glad that motherfucker dead. Maybe you will learn some respect from a real woman now, little girl."

Heavenly replies with a low but concerned voice, "Why would you say that about my father? Your sister was the one who was a whore and got him killed."

157

Theresa approaches Heavenly in a furious rage and she slaps her down to the ground. She stands over her and says, "Don't ever talk about my sister like that again. That is your mother. Your father hurt my sister over and over again, and she was still in love with his dirty ass, even after he left her with all of his children. So if you want to call someone a whore, it should be that piece of shit that you are protecting."

Heavenly lays there with tears in her eyes as Mark and Lindsey kneel down to soothe their sister. Theresa feels no remorse for her as she says, "Get your ass up and get these covers for you and your sister. Mark, come with me, baby. I will show you where you will be sleeping."

Heavenly gets up as she is mumbling under her breath that she hates her aunt and they will not be there for that long if she can help it. Heavenly always knew her aunt Theresa did not care much for her father, from what he had always told her, but she never knew the reason she didn't like him. Her mother always said her aunt Theresa was jealous that Julian was a good man and she could never find one like him, because she was so mean and rowdy. She was far from ladylike.

Heavenly and Lindsey are making the bed as she says, "Lindsey, don't listen to anyone but me about Dad. She doesn't even know him that well." She pulls the covers up on Lindsey. After they say their prayers, Heavenly tells her to go to sleep so she can go check on Mark.

As she is walking up the stairs, she hears water running. She notices her aunt Theresa is nowhere in sight, so she believes she is in the bathroom. She walks past the bathroom where Mark's room is. As she enters the room, she notices Mark has the covers pulled up to his eyes as if he is scared.

Heavenly gently pulls back the covers as she says, "It's me, Mark. Are you okay?"

Mark replies, "No, I'm scared someone might come kill me like they did Daddy."

Heavenly replies, "Did you pray like we always do at night? Because if you did, you know Daddy and God are watching over you, and you should not worry about anything."

Mark replies, "I know and I did pray, but it only works when you pray with me."

Heavenly says, "Close your eyes and we will silently pray with our hearts. Whether we are together or not, he knows what our heart desires and all our needs. So, don't think he does not hear your prayer."

Heavenly and Mark sit with their heads bowed in silence for over five minutes as they say together, "Amen." Heavenly gently kisses his forehead and says goodnight as she heads back to the family room with Lindsey. Heavenly leaves the room to go downstairs and she notices her aunt coming out of the bathroom.

Theresa grabs Heavenly by the arm and says, "You won't ruin those children as your father has ruined you, and if you even try, I will make sure you go visit your father faster than you would like to." Theresa releases Heavenly's arm and makes eye contact with her until she disappears down the stairs.

Heavenly gets in the bed with Lindsey and holds her close and very tight, as she lays there in her thoughts. She doesn't understand what has happened to her life and she can't do anything to save any of them. She feels so helpless. She drops a few tears and tries to get some rest.

*****

Theresa's phone rings and when she picks it up, she hears, "Collect call from New Orleans County Jail. Christine." The automated system says "Press 1 to accept the call," so Theresa accepts the call.

Theresa waits for Christine to get on the phone, then says, "Hello? Hey, little sis. How are you doing?"

Christine replies anxiously, "Do you know where my babies are at or who they are with? I gave them your information so they can tell you what's going on. Apparently, I have been charged with neglect, so they only told me that my kids were with the social worker."

Theresa replies, "Of course I know where they are. I have them all with me. That damn Heavenly is too much like her dad."

Christine says, "Don't do anything stupid and stop talking like that. You do know I have been charged with his murder. I just want to know, are they okay?"

Theresa replies, "Yes, they are okay and I will take good care of them. Do you have a court date, or can you have visitation?"

"I have an arraignment tomorrow morning and if I don't get out, you and the children can come and visit me for an emergency visit. Please be nice to my children. They have been through a lot. Thank you so much for taking them in, because I was afraid you would say no," Christine says.

The automated system prompts as they are finishing up the conversation. "You have sixty seconds before this call ends."

Theresa says as she is getting ready to end the call, "Hold your head up. I will be nice to the children. I love you, sis."

Christine replies, "I love you too, Theresa, and thank you again." The phone hangs up as Christine holds it her hand, wishing she was not in this predicament. She wants to at least speak to her children. She puts the phone on the receiver and walks away, going back to her cell.

*****

The next morning Theresa gets up and makes breakfast for her and the children. She goes to each room and awakens them so they can have breakfast. She says to the children as they come in the kitchen one by one, "Good morning, little people. I hope you slept well." They all just look at her and start eating. There is complete silence throughout the entire kitchen, except the sounds of their forks touching their plates and them chewing their food.

As everyone is eating, Theresa says, "So we will meet with Bonnie this morning and then we will be going to see your mother."

Heavenly looks at Theresa as if her food suddenly disgusts her. "I am not going to see her. They can go, but I will stay here."

Theresa holds up her hand as if she is going to say something sarcastic, but she suddenly drops it and says, "I refuse to leave you alone in my house. You definitely have no choice but to go and I will not be debating my decision with no children."

Heavenly replies, "Well, if you insist and I have no choice, I will go, but I am not visiting her at all."

Theresa ignores Heavenly's comment as she starts to wash the dishes she used to cook breakfast. While doing that, she mumbles under her breath. It took a lot for her not to knock that little girl out. "I don't like that little girl. Who the hell does she think she is? Who raised this grown ass woman? But for Christine, I am going to manage to be nice to her," Theresa says, encouraging herself to uphold her promise to her sister. She finishes the dishes and encourages the children to clean up their mess and get ready for the visit to see their mother.

*****

As Heavenly is helping Lindsey get dressed, she says to her, "No matter what happens, I love you and I will protect you always. My spirit will always be connected to you. Don't ever let your heart become mean or evil. Forgive anyone who hurts you. God will not like that kind of person who doesn't forgive. Understand you are a queen and you will always be my queen, and a daughter of your father God." She kisses Lindsey on the forehead and puts on her shirt.

Lindsey asks, "Heavenly, why is our aunt so mean? She's not a queen?"

Heavenly replies, "No, she is not a queen. She has an evil spirit. Pray for the demons to exit our life."

Lindsey agrees and walks out of the room to wait for Heavenly. Mark comes downstairs and then joins the both of them.

"This lady is coming here to either leave you with me or take you to some foster home until your mother gets out. So, you can agree to stay here or get out. Either way, I don't give a damn," Theresa says to the children as she pours some Cognac in a glass and sits on her chaise. She just stares at the children. As they are all sitting there looking confused, there is a sudden knock at the door and everyone looks at each other in surprise.

Theresa puts up the bottle of Cognac and runs to the bathroom to clean up. She says, "Heavenly, go open the door while I clean up this smell of the Cognac."

Heavenly opens the door and lets Bonnie the social worker into the house. As Bonnie enters the house, Theresa says, "Hello Bonnie, how are you today?"

Bonnie replies, "I am great, thanks for asking. You have a beautiful home."

"Thank you, I tried to make it comfortable for the children."

"Well, I came to see how the children are doing and to see your living arrangements," Bonnie says. "No rush, but it is more about business right now. Can you show me where the children will be sleeping and your food supply?"

Theresa looks at Bonnie and shakes her head in frustration as she says, "Come this way and I will show you where Mark sleeps. We will start upstairs."

Bonnie follows Theresa upstairs as she takes notes. She says, "This is a really nice room. It is definitely enough room for three people." They walk through the upstairs so she can check for smoke detectors and carbon monoxide monitors. They both walk downstairs as Bonnie continues to write notes about her findings and the condition of the home.

Theresa says as they are headed downstairs, "I have the girls sleeping downstairs in the family room. There is a pull-out couch in there."

Bonnie takes notes of the downstairs area where the girls sleep and she suddenly asks, "This is really nice and big as well, but where will the younger children play during the daytime?"

Theresa angrily replies, "I will have to move some things around, but I hope their mother is released and they will be home soon."

Bonnie writes her notes, then she says, "I now have to check your food supply and ask a few more questions, then the interview will be done."

Theresa walks Bonnie to the kitchen and shows her the refrigerator and cabinets, which are all full of food. Bonnie jots down more notes and then takes a seat at the kitchen table. She gestures for Theresa to do the same.

"How will you discipline the children if they do not obey your orders?"

Theresa replied, "I won't discipline them. I don't believe in punishing them because one day life will do that and then some."

Bonnie writes down Theresa's response on her notepad. "Do you have any addictions like alcohol, drugs, pills, etcetera?"

Theresa replied, "No, of course not. I am a law-abiding citizen who lives day to day, like everyone else."

Bonnie responds, "That's great to hear, but I did see an area in the dining room which looks like a setup for a bar. Do you use that area often?"

Theresa smiles to cover up frustration with Bonnie being so nosey. "When I have a family function, I do set up my bar to entertain my guests, and we both know that is not too often since it's only me and my sister."

Bonnie replies, "Well, it would be in your best interest to keep alcohol and anything else that's harmful out of the children's reach. We are pretty much done here. Here are the copies of the children's birth certificates. We will start a court petition for permanent custody. For now, here is proof they are in your temporary custody. Heavenly, Mark, and Lindsey, I hope your life gets better with time and that you have a pleasurable, healthy life with your aunt. Heavenly, here is my card in case you need anything."

Heavenly thanks Bonnie, as do Mark and Lindsey, and they return to their seats in the living room.

Theresa walks Bonnie to the door and Bonnie says, "I will check with you in a few months to see how the children are doing. You do know they will be watched closely because there was an open case days prior to their father's murder. Meanwhile, I think it's a great thing you're doing for the children," Bonnie says as she hands Theresa her business card.

Theresa replies as she is closing the door, "Thank you and we will be in touch with you if we have any questions."

Theresa completely closes the door and then walks back to the living room where the children are. "Well you little bastards can get ready to visit your mother. Wait a minute. You all really are bastards now that Julian is dead." Theresa stands in the doorway looking at the children as she laughs hysterically.

Heavenly becomes angry, but she knows not to show her emotions to her aunt, so she gathers both her siblings' coats to help them get ready for the visit. They are all quiet as they are scared to speak because of their aunt's emotionless response to their situation. Theresa turns on the radio and she dances around the house merrily until she receives a phone call. She lowers the radio and begins to have a conversation on the phone.

"Hey, baby. I haven't heard from you for a while. I am so glad to hear your voice," Theresa says.

The voice on the other end of the phone replies, "Boss lady, you heard what happened to your boy?"

Theresa replies, "Yes, of course I know what happened. I have his bastard ass kids with me now. I can't talk to you right now, but I can meet you at our usual spot. I will meet you there around 7:30 or 8:00 o'clock tonight. Does that time work for you?"

The person on the other end responds, "Yes, baby, that's cool. I will see you then. Oh, by the way, wear something sexy. You know, the usual outfit, boss lady."

Theresa smiles and hangs up the phone, satisfied with her phone conversation. Theresa and the kids proceed to walk out the door and get in the car for their drive to the visit.

Heavenly looks at her siblings on both sides of her and she notices they both are just staring out the window in a daze. She is trying to understand how this could have happened to these two because they are innocent. She can handle it, but they are so young. Heavenly wants to save Mark and Lindsey from anymore heartache, but it seems impossible, especially living with their Aunt Theresa or even being in her presence.

They finally arrive at the county jail. They park the car and follow the signs to the visitors' area. Heavenly grabs Mark and Lindsey's hands as they walk up to the visiting area doors.

They are all nervous, but they never utter one word as they walk in total silence, looking around at the secure area.

Theresa walks ahead of the children. She goes up to the desk and says, "I am here to visit Christine Valone. It's an emergency visit."

The deputy responds, "Okay, I need to see identification for you and anyone else who may have come with you to visit her."

Theresa passes the IDs for herself and all the children to the deputy as she begins to check them in. "Ma'am, only two children can come in at one time per visit. Are these your children?"

Theresa responds, "No, these are not my children. They are her children and she has three children, so they all can't come in the visit?"

The deputy replies, "Would you like to schedule a visit? You can come back if the visit has not been used."

Theresa responds, "No, I don't want to schedule a visit. I will just take the two younger children. The other one is old enough to wait out here until we are done."

The deputy responds, "Well, I will check you three in, but do you have a letter from their mother or a custody letter?"

Theresa replies, "I gave you the certified letter with the birth certificate."

The deputy signs them in and asks them to remove their jewelry, belts, hair pins and anything that is metal. She then instructs them to leave all their belongings in the locker as she hands Theresa two coins for the lockers. "When you are done putting away your belongings, come back to the desk and sign in for the visit. I will then show you where you will need to go from here," says the deputy.

They put their things away in the locker. Theresa turns to Heavenly and says, "You got your wish, little girl. Be a good little girl while we are gone."

Heavenly doesn't respond. She just holds her head down because deep inside, she wants to see her mother so she can know if she is doing good in this terrible situation. Theresa, Mark and Lindsey walk past Heavenly as if she is a stranger as they approach the desk for the visit.

"Okay, ma'am. You can follow me this way," the deputy says. The door buzzes as she opens it and guides them in. The door suddenly slams behind them and Mark falls to the floor, screaming for Lindsey to get down on the floor with him.

Theresa turns and looks at the both of them on the floor and says, "You two acting all crazy. Get your stupid asses up and stop embarrassing me in this place." She yanks them up one by one as if she is concerned. Two guards rush to the area where they are to make sure the children are okay. Theresa assures the deputies that the children are okay and they are ready for the visit with their mother. The deputies gesture for her and the children to go through the next set of doors and go to the visiting desk.

The deputy behind the visiting area desk asks Theresa, "Who are you coming to see?"

Theresa replies, "We are here to see Christine Valone for an emergency visit."

The deputy looks on the computer to see where she could seat them for the secure visit. Mark and Lindsey are holding each other tightly as they wait.

Mark whispers to Lindsey, "I wish Heavenly was here to protect us. I'm scared. This place is weird. What if they don't let us out and they keep us with Mommy?"

Lindsey responds softly, "Mark, Aunt Theresa is with us and Heavenly is only outside of the big door. And you know I will take care of you. They can't keep us. We didn't do anything. These people are criminals, including Mommy." Lindsey looks at Mark with a sad face and lays her head on his shoulder, as he squeezes her tight and pulls her closer.

They hear the deputy say, "You can go to cubicle 23 with the phone. Do not bang on the glass or yell. If any of this behavior is observed, the visit will be over immediately."

Theresa and the children go to the cubicle and await Christine's arrival.

"How are you two? I really miss you," Christine says when she arrives.

Mark replies, "We are okay, Mommy. We are staying at Auntie Theresa's house and it's really nice."

At first, Lindsey doesn't say anything. She holds her head down in complete sadness. Then she says, "Mom, Heavenly is outside and she couldn't come in."

Christine replies, "I know it's hard, but I am glad you all are with my sister. I hope to be out of here real soon, but listen to whatever she tells you. Why is Heavenly outside?"

Theresa replies, "Girl, I am glad the heathen didn't come in here. She wrecks my nerves."

Christine replies, "I know my children can be a lot, but Heavenly can help you with Mark and Lindsey. Give her a chance, Theresa. Please. For me."

Theresa replies, "You need to hurry up and get out so we can finish what we started."

Christine looks at Theresa as if she sees something awful on her face and she says, "Don't you dare talk that way in front of my children, or anyone else."

Theresa laughs hysterically. "You were always so damn sensitive, and that's why your ass is in here now."

Christine shakes her head as she replies, "Listen, I can't discuss anything in here. This stuff is recorded even though I am innocent. I cannot discuss my case. But, sensitive? Never. Compassionate? Always. Please know the difference. Besides, be mindful how you treat my children because your animosity can ruin everything." Christine stares deep into Theresa's eyes so she can hear and feel the words Christine just spoke to her.

Lindsey and Mark sit there looking confused. They don't know if they are fighting or just having a conversation, so each time either one of them speaks, they just follow the conversation.

The deputy suddenly screams across the room "23, Valone, the visit is over. Time is up. Your 30 minutes are over."

Another guard comes to the cubicle and tells them to wrap it up. Theresa says with a smirk on her face, "I got a phone call before I came here and he seemed a tad bit unusual, but you know me and him always goes through this love thing. Anyways, I will look after your lovely children, and is there something you want me to tell Heavenly?"

Christine replies, "Yes, tell her I love her and I am very sorry for everything. And please find it in her heart to forgive me." They all get up and put their hands on the glass and blow kisses in a manner of saying good bye. Christine yells through the glass, "Momma loves you and I will see you soon. Theresa, please try to get me out of here before my court date. Try to bail me out."

Theresa and the children walk away from the cubicle and they exit the visiting room. They get to the waiting area and Mark and Lindsey run up to Heavenly and start squeezing her tight. Theresa is at the desk waiting for their identification and the keys to the locker.

Heavenly says, "How was the visit, and what did Mommy say?"

Mark replies, "She didn't say much to us, but the visit was okay."

Lindsey says, "No, mom and Aunt Theresa seem like they were fighting and I think Mommy told her off. So, I think it went bad, plus we didn't stay that long."

Heavenly asks, "Well, what were they talking about? What they said?"

Lindsey replies, "Mommy seemed like she was mad, and told Aunt Theresa not to play her and that she will mess her up. Aunt Theresa said something about a plan and a phone call from her boyfriend. Oh, and Mommy said she loves you and she's sorry."

Heavenly says, "Do not repeat this to anyone else. You pinky promise?"

"Yes, I pinky promise, sister," Lindsey replies.

They both look over at Mark and he says, "I am not going to say anything to anybody."

Heavenly says, "Shh, Aunt Theresa is on her way over here. You guys know how to pretend like we are having a different conversation. Let's practice now."

Theresa walks up and says, "What are you three snakes talking about? I bet you are talking about me." Theresa proceeds to walk past them. The children turn around and walk out the door behind Theresa.

Theresa unlocks the car doors and lets them into the car. She texts someone before they pull out the parking lot. The text reads, "Call me now. I am done with my visit."

She receives a phone call not long after she sent the text. She picks up the phone when she hears it ring. "Hello, meet me at our favorite place where you can have all you can eat," Theresa says as she chuckles. I need to prepare, so give me a little while. I got to drop these kids off and get them situated."

Heavenly is in the back seat trying to make sense of the conversation. She can clearly hear a man's voice on the phone, but they have never seen her with a man or heard of her having a man from what their parents had told them. Heavenly suddenly falls into a daze as she stares out the window, trying to think of whom this man could be or where he came from.

CHAPTER TEN

~ The Surprise ~

Charlene lays there holding Julian's pillow, weeping and continuously sniffing his fragrance. Her heart and tears become heavier. She stares at the letters and pictures that surround her and remind her of Julian. Julian had written those letters in response to her leaving letters for him to read, because Charlene did not know how to communicate very well except on paper. She looks over at the dresser through her misty eyes and spots the pregnancy test she had bought earlier. She says, "Lord, I hope this is not happening to me again."

She slowly gets up and walks toward the dresser. She grabs the pregnancy test and stumbles to the bathroom. She feels weak and tired from crying, but she enters the bathroom with the assistance of holding onto the wall for support. Charlene just stands there and looks at the test, hesitating to open it up. "I am not sure if I want know. Lord, help me from any more pain," Charlene says as she attempts to have a seat on the edge of the tub, almost sliding off. She holds her head down and continues to weep even harder.

180

She holds the test in her hands and she falls into a long, deep stare as she thinks of the past. The whole scene has brought back unwanted memories and emotions, which was the same reason she broke it off with Julian. She begins to slowly open the test and a strange feeling overcomes her. She just drops the box on the floor as she says, "Julian is that you? Are you here with me? I can feel your presence. Just speak to me, please." She falls to the floor in the fetal position next to the test, as she just stares at it and cries profusely. "I can't do this again without you. Why did you leave me again? Why me? Why me?" she screams through her weakened cries.

She turns her focus back on the pregnancy test and begins opening the box again. She grabs the tub to balance herself so she can sit up on the toilet to take the test. As she is unfolding the wrapping around the test, she suddenly feels the urge to urinate. She clenches to stop the urge. A feeling of nervousness comes upon her and she begins to shake. She takes a deep breath, places the test in position, and begins to flow upon the test strip. She feels her flow come to an end and she places the test on the edge of the sink. As she begins to wipe herself clean, she stares at the test as if she is scared to touch it. With every stroke of wiping herself she visualizes her last encounter with Julian and a stream of tears begins to roll down her cheeks. She pulls up her undergarments and stands in front of the sink, looking in the mirror so she can avoid looking at the test.

"God, why did you give me this life? I have no chance of living a good life. Why have you forsaken me?" She just stares at herself in the mirror and then decides to look down at the test. As her eyes land on the test, they widen and dilate as she says, "No, this cannot be right. I don't need this right now."

Charlene screams at the top of her weakened lungs. In disbelief, she stares at the test and the two lines that have appeared, showing a positive pregnancy result. "Julian's dead. What can I do with a baby?" She touches her stomach gently and starts rubbing it up and down to feel some sort of connection with the baby. As she continues to rub her stomach, the touches go from gentle to aggressive as she begins to become angry. "I can't have this baby with no father to help me raise it."

She begins feeling more and more angry, crying as she thinks of being pregnant. She suddenly stops rubbing her stomach and in a rage of pure violence, she starts punching her stomach to harm the baby. After ten hard blows to the stomach, she feels a sudden burst of cramps in her stomach, which bring her to her knees. As she kneels down in great pain, she begins to regret her actions. She slowly stands to her feet, holding onto the sink for assistance. Charlene is in great pain as she stumbles from the bathroom to the bedroom and falls upon the bed.

"Julian, I am so sorry, baby. I can't do this without you and you are never coming back." She wraps her arms around his picture as if she is hugging Julian himself. She lays there with tears running down her face from all the pain she has had to endure from Julian's death, the break up, and now the pregnancy that he didn't know anything about. "Lord, I just want the pain to stop."

She slowly rises up off the bed and walks toward the dresser. She opens the dresser drawer and takes a long look at what the dresser drawer contains. She moves a few things around and she runs across her prescription drugs. She picks up each bottle to identify what drug each one contains. She grabs one of the bottles and closes the drawer. She begins to walk to the other side of the room in search of something. She approaches the shelf and looks on top of each one until she finds what she is looking for—a pen and a notebook. She places the pen and notebook on the bed and exits the room slowly. Charlene walks to the kitchen, turns on the faucet, and gets a glass out the cabinet to get a glass of water. She takes the glass of water and returns to the room. Charlene sits the glass of water on the dresser and turns to pick up the pen and notebook. She begins to write a letter to Julian as she places his picture close to her:

Dear Julian,

I hope you see this letter and feel how much pain is in my heart right now. I miss you already, my love. I remember when we first met. All I could see was your beautiful smile, but when you spoke, there were great words to match that beautiful smile that I fell in love with instantly. We were best friends and lovers at all times. When we had sex for the first time, I felt like my whole heart opened up. I was so vulnerable to your love from that point on. I wanted to be vulnerable because we were so much alike in so many different ways. I cherished the fact that you loved God unconditionally and so did I. When things were hard for me with my family, you prayed with me and kept me laughing. My mind was so at ease anytime I was around you.

Then something happened. I don't even know what happened, but you left me with no fair warning. My heart was so heavy. You wouldn't answer my calls, and you didn't return them either. This broke my spirit, as if I had died but was still alive. I cried all day and night, trying to forget all about you, but I couldn't. When I heard you were with Christine, my soul died. I was so torn to pieces because I was thinking you really loved me the way I loved you, but I was wrong. I became bitter and angry, wanting to hurt you the same way you hurt me. After days of thinking about it, I decided to take my life. How would you feel if I left you with the burden of my death on your hands? I waited until no one was home and took a bottle of pills. As I slowly drifted away, all I could see was that beautiful smile and you there praying for me. When I awoke in the hospital, I learned that I lost the baby and I became depressed. I wasn't even aware that I was pregnant. I didn't want to tell you so you can pretend that you love me again, so I went to counseling and have been taking medication ever since. When I heard Christine was also pregnant, it sent me back to the hospital.

This time, I vowed to get you out my system for good by any means necessary. I pretended like I was okay around other people, but by myself, I would weep in the late hours of the night when my mother was sleeping. I never truly got over my love for you. When you returned to my life, it was not the same.

I have so much love for you, but I was afraid to feel hopeless again. I lied to you and treated you badly because I just couldn't give you that much power again. I hope you forgive me because you are the love of my life. I hope you are in heaven with our first child, and you will now get a chance to be with us as a family. I love you Julian. Me and our second child will see you on the other side real soon.

Love always—your first true love,

Charlene Valone

Charlene places the letter next to Julian's picture, and then reaches for the glass of water and the prescription drugs. As she weeps, she twists off the bottle top and pours numerous pills into her hand. Charlene stares at the pills, contemplating whether or not these pills should be taken. Suddenly she puts the glass up to her mouth, sipping the water in small increments. She opens her mouth and places all the pills in her mouth. She takes a big gulp of water, assisting the pills in going down her throat. As she places the glass of water on the dresser, she returns to the bed. Charlene lies on the pillow that smells just like Julian's cologne as she places the letter next to the picture beside her. She smiles at the idea of seeing him again, as he will be at complete peace now that they are on the way to see him.

*****

Meanwhile at the precinct, Jean and Steve are going over the details of Julian's murder. "Steve, have you read Tony and Simon's report?" Jean asks.

Steve replies, "No, I have not. Is there something in particular you want me to look at?"

"I personally believe Andrew is telling the truth, but how can we prove Christine was involved? There wasn't any identification found at her home, except for the people who live there," Jean says.

"If you do pursue this, right now we only have circumstantial evidence. Besides, Shawn already gave a full confession to the crime."

Jean replies, "Well, that is only one of our problems. The other is we have to go tell Charlene that her brother killed her boyfriend. She may also have some other information, which Julian may have told her about Christine. I will give you a little time to read the report before we head over to Charlene's house."

Steve continues to read the report, and then he says to Jean, "You do know that there is something strange about Andrews's statement. There are many possibilities in his theory, but there is no record of an Angie Ruiz."

Jean replies, "Listen, I will find out who is the link to Slim. This has to be connected from the inside somehow, but for now, we are going to see what Charlene has to say about this whole thing. Charlene does know about the murder, but I know she will be devastated to find out her cousin and brother were plotting to kill him all along. You can see she really cares about Julian, and it's all a sad case, stemming from her attempting suicide years ago. She was a young girl that was just confused and in love with the wrong person. I truly hope this doesn't send her backwards."

*****

Jean and Steve pull up to Charlene's home and take a look at each other before they both exit the car. As they walk up the driveway, they notice the music is on and all the lights are on as well. They begin knocking on the door. Their knocks are unanswered, so they knock even harder.

"I don't think anyone is here," Steve says.

Jean replies, "Someone is in there. Don't you hear that music? She can't hear us through the music."

Steve says, "I'll go to the front of the house and knock while you stay here and knock. She is sure to hear one of us."

Jean nods her head yes and continues to knock. A sudden feeling comes over Jean and she stops knocking on the door and runs to the front where Steve is knocking. "Steve, I have a very bad feeling about this whole scene. I was on the scene when Charlene tried to commit suicide years ago, and this just feels weird, like something is wrong. If no one comes to the door, we are going in."

Steve replies, "We don't have a warrant. That would be illegal and I will not participate in this."

Jean replies, "It won't be illegal if she is in there and in trouble. For God's sake, I'm going in. My intuition won't let me wait for a warrant, and so do as you please. I will go alone." Jean looks at the front door to see if it is weak enough to be kicked in, but it looks really sturdy. She also turns the knob to see if it is open, but it isn't. She walks around to the side door and turns the knob, and to her surprise, it is unlocked.

She opens the door and looks around, screaming Charlene's name. "Charlene, Charlene," she calls out as she scrambles through the house looking from room to room. She rapidly runs up the stairs to check for Charlene, but she is not there. She runs back downstairs and goes through the house, still calling her name.

As she approaches the bedroom, she spots Charlene lying on the bed seeming to be sleep. She calls her name as she turns down the radio. She notices Charlene doesn't respond, so she checks her pulse and her breathing. Her pulse is very faint, but she is still breathing which means she is alive.

When Jean touches her, Charlene barely opens her eyes and says very softly, "Julian, you came back for me."

Jean yells, "Charlene, stay with me, baby girl." Jean pulls out her phone and calls for an ambulance as a tear drops down her cheek. "I need an ambulance for a possible suicide. This is detective Jean. Please hurry. I don't know how long she has been here or what she took, but she has shallow breathing and a very shallow pulse."

Jean gently lays Charlene back on the bed and runs to the bathroom to see if she can find what Charlene has taken. As she approaches the bathroom sink, she sees the pregnancy test on the sink as she says, "Not again. I can't let her lose this one too." As she is walking out of the bathroom, she looks up and notices the empty glass and bottle of pills on the dresser.

Suddenly, she hears someone calling her name, "Jean, Jean, are you okay? I heard the call over the radio. Is she still alive?"

Jean walks over to the dresser to take a closer look at the bottle. "Valium. She has a possibility of surviving. I don't think it can kill her, but it depends on how much she took and whether she took anything else with it."

As Jean is talking to Charlene to keep her somewhat alert, she notices the ambulance lights and runs to go get them and bring them inside to Charlene. Jean says to the paramedics, "I am detective Jean. The scene is secure and my partner is inside with the patient."

Jean looks up to the sky and says, "God, I know I have not been obedient, but I know you answer prayers. This woman has been through so much. Touch her life, oh Holy Spirit. Please save her."

Jean then turns around and notices the EMTs rushing her to the ambulance. She asks, "Which hospital will you be taking her to?"

"Saint Mohawk Regional Hospital," the paramedic replies.

"Thank you. I will meet you at the hospital," Jean says. Steve and Jean get in the car and follow the ambulance to the hospital.

As Steve and Jean are in the waiting room awaiting the results from the doctor, Jean says, "In all my years as a detective, the only thing that bothers me is suicide."

She walks over to the window and, with a blank stare, says to Steve, "When I was ten, my father left my mother and I was not aware of it because he came home every night. What I didn't realize was he only stayed until me and my siblings fell asleep. All along, he had another family, but he didn't want us to suffer from his actions, so they came up with a plan to hide it from us. Their plan did more damage to my mother and I would hear them argue sometimes at night. One night, I was up when they were arguing and it was so intense, I knew something was wrong. I went to the top of the stairs because it got really quiet all of a sudden and then I heard the door shut closed. I saw my mother crying so hard, I wanted to hug her, but unfortunately I didn't. I prayed to God to help my mother, but a moment later, she came in and kissed me on my forehead and said, 'I love you, my little angel. Don't ever stop praying and believing in the good of God. I stopped believing and now I am sick.' I felt relieved that God had answered my prayers. She was going to be okay. The next morning when we got up, I found a note and my mother lying next to it. She had committed suicide because of the hurt she had from my dad leaving. I still believe that God works miracles, but I was angry and stepped away from church for years now."

Steve moves closer to Jean as he says, "I am so sorry to hear that, Jean. I see why it has become personal for you. Maybe you can take a leave of absence and be taken off the case."

Jean replies, "I will be fine. I am a big girl with a job to do. Maybe God put me in this position so I can save others from actually committing suicide. He positioned me for the position."

Steve replies, "Yea, I guess so, but if it is too much, then promise me you will take that leave of absence."

Looking out the window with a blank stare, Jean says, "Sure. I will if it becomes too much for me."

CHAPTER ELEVEN
~ The Great Revenge ~

"I will be gone for a little while, so be good and listen to your sister. Heavenly, fix them something to eat and put them to bed. Please don't wait up. Bedtime is at eight o'clock. Oh, Heavenly, since you are a teenager you can choose when you go to bed. Just don't have your ass up when I get here." Theresa gets a shot of Cognac, grabs her keys, and heads out the door.

Heavenly goes to the kitchen to figure out what they are going to eat for dinner. She knows what she will prepare and goes to the living room to see if Lindsey and Mark are okay with it. "Aunt Theresa had some hamburger meat thawed out. Do you want spaghetti and a tossed salad?" Heavenly asks. They both respond to Heavenly's questions as they nod yes. Heavenly encourages them to watch TV while she makes dinner. "Do not argue over the remote and do not jump on the couches. If I catch you doing either of those things I will send you to bed early. Understood?"

Mark and Lindsey shake their heads in unison as they say, "Yes, Heavenly, we understand." Heavenly proceeds to the kitchen to cook dinner, as Lindsey and Mark sit quietly and watch TV.

*****

"I am on my way to our special spot. I hope you have a surprise for me as you usually do," Theresa says.

"Of course, baby. I definitely got to do something special for you because you are definitely a queen," says the person on the other end of the phone.

"I am about to pull up now. I will be waiting for you, Daddy," Theresa says. Theresa pulls up to the hotel, exits the car, and proceeds to go get a room.

"Hello, can I help you, Mrs. Newman?" the receptionist at the desk asks.

"Yes, I would like the normal suite. Is it available? I would have called, but I was kind of busy today," Theresa says.

"Let me take a look and see if it is available," the receptionist says as she searches the computer for the suite

Theresa prefers. "Mrs. Newman, your suite is available. Would you like to charge it to your account?"

"That would be perfect. Just send my usual guest upstairs and give me a buzz that he is on the way. Thank you," Theresa says as she walks to the elevator. Theresa goes to the room to prepare for the arrival of her guest and to put her things away.

"I am here to see Mrs. Newman," the guest says to the receptionist.

"She is in Suite B as usual, sir," the receptionist says.

"Thank you. I will head up there now," the guest says.

"Mrs. Newman, your guest is on the way up," the receptionist says.

Theresa replies, "Thank you," as she hangs up the phone and awaits her guest. Theresa hears a knock and walks over to answer the door. As she looks through the keyhole, she asks, "Who is it?"

The man replies, "The love of your life, the one who always holds you down."

Theresa replies sarcastically, "It's impossible for me to be on both sides of the door."

The man says, "Just open the door, woman, please and thank you."

Theresa opens the door and gives the man a big, long hug and kiss on the cheek. "I missed you. With so much that has happened in my life, it's a relief to see you"

The man replies to Theresa, "Do you really miss me? Have you been keeping things in order for Daddy?"

Theresa walks over to the bar and pours them both a drink of Cognac, and then passes the man his drink. "So, you heard what happened to Julian, and that they have my sister Christine in jail for his murder. So, what I understand is they have Slim and Andrew in custody as well, but my concern is will they trace anything back to me?"

The man responds, "Why would you say that, Queen? We don't have anything to do with that. Slim killed that dude and we both know he had it in for this guy for a long time."

Theresa smiles at the man, grabs his hand, and starts gently stroking it as she says, "You put him in the game under my orders. Christine is my little sister, Julian is dead, and what if Slim turns on both of us? If I go down, a lot of big dogs will not be happy that their money has been cut short, so you better hope he is loyal. But who really is nowadays?" Theresa goes over to the bar and pours herself another shot of cognac.

The man replies, "Theresa, Slim is from the hood. He will not snitch, but what I don't know is how his cousin moves or how much he has told him. I promise you, I bet my life on Slim's loyalty. Your sister and that cousin is the fucking issue."

Theresa replies with a chuckle. "My sister, she will not say anything and I know she didn't tell Andrew anything. So, with all that being said, stay low and off the scene just in case." Theresa walks over to the sofa and sits as she sips her drink. The man begins to walk toward the door to exit the room, but Theresa catches his attention and says, "Oh, by the way, didn't you forget the main reason we are here, Reggie?"

Reggie pulls the money out of the lining of his jacket and hands it to Theresa. Reggie says to Theresa, "I need that shipment by Friday. It may move slower than usual because of the cops lingering around the neighborhood."

Theresa jumps up and walks toward Reggie in a slow stride as she says, "You know how to make money. Don't let that be the reason you don't make money." She lightly kisses Reggie on the cheek and then turns to go sit back on the couch.

Reggie stands there in disbelief. He has been working for Theresa for many years and has always been loyal. He stares at Theresa, turns, and walks toward the door. He takes a few seconds to look back over his shoulder, as if he felt she would shoot him in the back right there on the spot. Theresa just blows a kiss at Reggie and takes another sip of her drink. Reggie shakes his head and walks out of the room.

As Reggie exits the room, Theresa picks up the phone and makes a call. "Low, how are you, baby?"

Low replies, "I am great and it's definitely is pleasant to hear from you, Queen."

"That's always good to hear, Low," Theresa says, "I really need to check on our cousin Reggie. He is going through a lot so keep an eye on him. Pay him a visit to make sure he is alright."

Low replies, "You know family comes first always, my Queen. I will definitely check on Cuz. I don't want him to

make a bad choice and then lose everything, so I will definitely
hold you down and check up on him—show some support. I
will check on him tomorrow, or should I check on him
tonight?"

Theresa says, "He seemed okay when he left, but please
go by there tomorrow and make sure he is still okay."

"Okay I will hit you up tomorrow and tell you how cuz
is doing," Low promises.

Theresa replies, "Great, talk to you later." Theresa and
Low hang up the phone. She lies on the bed and begins to
count the the money that Reggie had given to her.

*****

Reggie gets in the car and turns it on. He picks up his
phone to make a phone call as he says, "Baby, where you at?"

The women replies, "I am home where you left me.
Why, what's up, Bae?'

"Listen, it's crunch time right now," Reggie says.

The women asks, "Okay, are we making it happen now
or later?"

Reggie replies, "Right now. The Queen is acting real strange. I think she is overwhelmed with all the things that are going on in her life right now. You know when she is concerned about the family she will send Low to check on them. You know Low will rob you of your soul, so I don't want to be bothered with him and what he stands for. I am on my way, so clean the house real good and put everything in place, just in case we have an uninvited guest. Love you."

Reggie continues to drive. He arrives to the local neighborhood where he and his roommates reside. As he exits the car, he feels the vibration of his phone and he answers it. "Hello."

The voice on the other end says, "Hello, Reggie."

Reggie recognizes the voice and says, "Are you okay? I heard what has happened and I know you need to talk, beautiful. The person on the other end says, "Yes, I am fine, but can I come over? I have a lot to say and it just seems like no one is listening."

Reggie replies, "Give me a few minutes and I will meet you so we can talk."

The person on the other end of the phone replies, "How long will that be? I don't have much time to get back home."

Reggie replies, "Heavenly, you have to trust me. I won't be long, baby girl."

Heavenly replies, "Okay, meet me at the four corners in twenty minutes."

Reggie replies, "Cool, I will be there. I got some business to handle."

They hang up the phone and Heavenly gets ready to meet with Reggie.

*****

Meanwhile, Reggie walks into the house where his roommates are at. "Yo, where everybody at?" Reggie asks.

His roommate replies, "Those other two are upstairs. What's up?"

Reggie replies, "Yo, we got to shut down for a little while. The Queen is sending Low and you definitely know what that means. I am going to get this shit off and give her money and be done for good. She acting real strange, yo."

The roommate replies, "Why the fuck would she send Low? He the hit man. What the hell you done and we don't know anything about it?"

Reggie replies, "First of all, I met with her a little while ago and she thinks Slim or Andrew are going to snitch, which puts me and her in jeopardy of being involved with old boy murder. We cannot afford that kind of heat or get arrested because people are snitching. I told her Slim is from around the way, but I really don't know much about Andrew. So I advise you motherfuckers to find somewhere to lay low and be still for a while. I came to warn you dudes that she sent out Low to clean up any loose ends, but I am about to disappear, make this money, and get out of the game. This shit is too much, but you be safe. I got to meet someone, but I'm out of here. I will holla at you later, check up on you dudes." Reggie slaps up each one of the roommates and exits the house.

As Reggie walks out of the house, he looks down to see the time on his phone and notices twenty-five minutes have passed by already. He jumps in his car to race over to four corners to meet Heavenly.

*****

"Lindsey and Mark, it's time for bed. Say your prayers and please lie down. I will be leaving for a little while. Don't come out of the room unless you are together. Keep the phone in the bed with you, and if Aunt Theresa asks where I am, tell her I took a walk," Heavenly says as she walks Mark and Lindsey upstairs to the bedroom and kisses them on their foreheads.

"I will lock the door behind me. I have the key and Aunt Theresa does as well, so if you hear anything strange, call 911," Heavenly says as she starts to close the door and exit the room.

As she walks out the door on her way to meet Reggie, she notices a car slowly driving past. She gets nervous and stares deep into the car and notices it come to a complete stop. As she walks closer to the passing car, she looks to see if she knows the person. She realizes it is Reggie, so she hurries to the car so she won't be noticed.

"How did you know where I was at? I told you to meet me at four corners," Heavenly says.

Reggie replies, "I know more than you think I know, baby girl."

"Whatever, dude. How have you been?" Heavenly asks.

"I have been good, but a lot has been on my mind," Reggie says. "When you called, I realized someone else had it worst than me. How have you been with everything that's going on? I mean, I heard what happened to your father."

Heavenly replies, "Yea, it's been rough for me, Mark, and Lindsey. I know something isn't right because my father didn't have any enemies. I just want an answer as to why they had to kill him."

As Reggie is listening to Heavenly, he looks over at her in the passenger seat and notices tears coming down her face. He says, "If you don't mind, I will go somewhere that is comfortable for both of us and we can sit and talk."

"That's fine. Just get me away from here. By the way, how did you know where I was at again?"

Reggie replies, "I didn't know. I came through this area to get to four corners. As I was passing by, I saw you coming out of the house and I just slowed down, then stopped. You know things have a reason for happening. It may not be clear now, but you will see in the future. I know you are going through a difficult time, but you should pray for the rest of your family's well-being."

Heavenly replies, "Me, Mark and Lindsey are the only ones that I consider family. My mom, I love her, but I blame her for some of the things we have gone through. My aunt is a terrible person. She seems like she hates us and honestly, I don't know why. My dad is gone and he was the very person who kept me with some hope in my life. This all can't be real. My life is a total mess and I have no control over it. I graduate in a few weeks, and I just want to go to college and forget this town and whoever is in it."

Reggie finds a spot, pulls over in the local shopping center, and parks. He says to Heavenly, "I know at your age these things can be hard to deal with, but you have to believe it will get better with time. I am going to tell you something, but I need you promise me you will keep it to yourself."

Heavenly looks at Reggie and says, "You are my only true friend. Everyone else talks about my dad and me like we are so evil. You can trust me with your life."

At that moment, Reggie knows he has Heavenly wrapped around his finger, but now he has to figure out a way to put his plan into effect. He says, "Heavenly, I am leaving this town. It is no longer has the value it used to have, so I need to leave and start all over." He grabs Heavenly's hand and holds it as if he is saying goodbye right now.

Heavenly holds his hand tighter as she says, "Reggie, please take me with you. I want to start over too."

Reggie looks at her as he grabs her face and says, "Baby girl, how can I do that when you are so young? They will be looking for you. I don't need any more cases on me. How will I keep in contact with you, if I did decide to take you with me?"

Heavenly replies, "You can buy me a cell phone and we can text and call every night. I will hide the phone so no one knows that have it."

Reggie looks up and notices Wal-Mart in the plaza where they had parked, and he says, "I am going to go in here and buy you a minute phone, and I will buy you some extra cards so you will never run out of minutes. Stay here, turn on the radio if you want to, but don't get out of the car."

Heavenly replies, "Okay, I will wait for you to come back."

Reggie exits the car with a smile on his face as he puts Phase One of his plan into play. With a big smile on her face, Heavenly sits in the car and listens to the radio as she daydreams about a life with just her and Reggie.

Reggie purchases the cell phone and is now headed back to the car. As he gets in the car, he hands Heavenly the cell phone and says to her, "Call me now so I can store your number in my phone. So, when you call, I can answer and I will be only answering phone calls that I know from now on."

Heavenly turns on the phone and calls Reggie's phone. She is excited and feels very important to him.

"I am about to drop you back off before they start looking for you. You're not eighteen yet," Reggie says as they both chuckle. Reggie drives Heavenly near her home and says, "I will text you later. I have some things to take care of first, but I will be in touch."

Before Heavenly gets out of the car, she looks at Reggie and realizes she is attracted to him still. As she leans over to hug him, she gives him a gentle, warm kiss on the lips and says goodbye.

Reggie watches her disappear around the corner. He's confused by Heavenly's actions. He breaks out of the element of surprise as he picks up his phone and makes a call. "Baby, you took care of that? Because I need you to go visit your mother in Florida for a little while."

The woman responds, "Yes, I handled that and cool. I need a vacation anyways."

Reggie replies, "I am on my way so I can take you to the airport. Call your mother and let her know the both of you are coming. By the way, tell her I said hello and I will take good care of her for doing this favor for us."

He hangs up the phone as he smiles about everything that has fallen into play. He says, "This bitch thinks she's running shit. I'm going to have this little bitch about to be eating out of my hand. Who the fuck do she think I am? Don't play with me, bitch."

*****

As Heavenly walks in the door, she notices her Aunt Theresa sitting at the dining room table, sipping on her glass of Cognac as she always does. She knows Theresa is going to say something to her, so she has to think quickly.

Theresa sees Heavenly walking in slowly and she knows Heavenly has seen her sitting there. "Where the hell you been, little girl?" Theresa asks.

Heavenly replies, "When they went to sleep, I decided to take a walk, Auntie. I am so sorry. I didn't know what else to do."

Theresa replies, "It's late for a little innocent girl to be out here. Take your behind to bed and don't try that shit again." Theresa finishes the last sip of her drink as she begins to talk out loud and say, "I have more things to worry about than some damn grown ass kids. I think I will go bail their mother out. This shit is too much." She puts the glass in the sink and proceeds to turn off all the lights as she heads upstairs to go to bed.

CHAPTER TWELVE

~ The Goddess ~

Theresa gets up and takes Mark and Lindsey to school, and then heads to court for Christine's arraignment. As she enters the courtroom parking lot, she notices she is receiving a phone call and she picks it up, "Hello, who is this? Because I don't recognize this number."

"Well hello, Queen. I heard you sent our cousin to see me. Did you think I was stupid? I have been dealing with you for too long, but I can tell you this much: Know who you fucking with, Princess."

Reggie hangs up the phone and leaves Theresa angry and confused as she says out loud, "That motherfucker done lost his mind. I will kill his whole fucking family. I was just going to kill him, but I am wiping all his family out since he wants to test me."

She continues to walk up the courthouse steps to see Christine's appearance in court. As she enters the courtroom, she notices that Slim is at the podium and he leaves with no bail. They call Christine up next and the judge gives her $200,000 bail because she is not a flight risk. Christine turns around and notices Theresa in the courtroom. She nods her head and is escorted back to jail.

Theresa leaves the courthouse and gets on the phone with her accountant. "I need $200,000 from my real estate company account, and make the check payable to New Orleans County. I need to bail Christine out of jail. How long before you can have that check ready for me?"

The accountant responds, "Give me about two hours and I will meet you down there at the courthouse."

Theresa replies, "That is perfect for me. I have a few things to handle myself."

Theresa hangs up the phone and calls Low. "I know you haven't seen or talked to our favorite cousin, but I believe it's a genocide about to happen, so I need you to check on the family history for me."

Low responds, "I will have a whole history of the information for you later, and I won't stop until I retrieve all the information I need to make sure the genocide does not happen."

Theresa responds, "You have always been so concerned about the family. I truly admire the loyalty you show to those you love. Give me a call later to let me know how far you got on that information." She hangs up the phone with a big smile and plenty of relief because she knows Low will kill anything that gets in her way.

*****

"Hey, can you pick me up by the school or I can go to the plaza? I don't feel like going to school today. I have a half day anyways."

Reggie replies, "Tell me your location and give me a few minutes, but stay out of sight."

Heavenly says, "Okay. I am going to go to Subway and wait for you. I am going to be in the plaza where you brought me last night." Heavenly hangs up the phone and starts to walk towards the plaza where Subway is so she can wait for Reggie.

Reggie lies in the bed, looking at the ceiling. He starts thinking to himself as he says, "I see she is going to make this a little bit harder than I expected. I got to let her know she cannot be skipping school and shit."

He jumps up to get in the shower and throw on some sweatpants and a tee shirt. He gets out of the shower, gets dressed, and heads out the door to go get Heavenly. He notices she is calling him back. Reggie answers the phone and says, "Listen, you are going to have to learn to be patient. I am on my way."

*****

What Reggie doesn't know is Heavenly can't stop thinking about him and being together. She has plans of her own and is very anxious to see Reggie and tell him about her plans. As Reggie pulls up to the Subway, Heavenly notices him and she comes out with a big smile on her face. In contrast, Reggie is a little agitated with Heavenly's sudden aggressiveness.

"Why are you looking like that, Reggie? Is there something wrong?" Heavenly asks.

Reggie replies, "There is something wrong. You cannot be skipping school and calling me to pick you up in the broad daylight. No one should be able to connect you and me together if you are serious about leaving with me."

Heavenly's mood suddenly changes as she feels that Reggie is rejecting her. She says, "I am sorry. I was very excited about leaving this town and I was feeling a little down. Seeing your face, hearing your voice cheers me up."

Reggie replies, "I apologize if I seemed harsh, but I just want you to know, if we are seen together they can come looking for me and they will find you at the same time. More so for you, it's about being more careful."

Heavenly smiles as she says, "I do understand. I will be more careful."

Reggie nods his head to accept Heavenly's confirmation as he turns up the radio for the rest of the ride to the hotel.

*****

"Girl, you are lucky we are family. You have to go home and get cleaned up. I can't be associated with a jail bird," Theresa says as she looks at Christine in disgust.

Christine replies, "I am just glad to be out of that cell. Jail is definitely not for me. I need to go to my house and get some clothes. I can't stay there because I am not ready to relive

216

that whole scene. Are all the kids at school? Because I want to surprise them as they come home."

Christine and Theresa walk to the car and get in. They begin to travel over to Christine's house.

"Let me ask you something," Theresa says. "Have you told anyone besides Slim about our plans? Because I sent Low over to Reggie's because you know I don't trust no one. Your little lover, Slim, will get dealt with as well if he even utters one wrong name."

Christine looks at Theresa in disbelief because she has forgotten the reason she had involved Slim in the first place; he hated Julian more than the both of them. Christine replies, "Why would he put other people's names in it when he got what he wanted? My lawyer said that he gave a full confession to everything and he only used me and Andrew to get to Julian. So, he is trying to get my charges reduced to expugnable probation, which means I won't get any more days in jail if it all falls through. Man, I am so tired of playing the loving wife. I can't wait to be able to rejoice that he's fucking dead." Christine and Theresa begin to laugh after she made that comment.

Theresa responds, "Well I trust you, so I will not send anyone after Slim for now. That damn Reggie. I want his head and his whole family's heads."

Christine shakes her head as she replies, "I don't understand why Reggie was involved anyways."

Theresa glances over at Christine as she says, "How else could I have helped your little lover out? I personally could not put him on. Shit, as far as people really know, I am just a myth that runs the street from my living room. I would never risk taking that chance of being connected to him. Look where he's at now. He was too impatient because he could have done the same thing, but been waiting on you to come home." Theresa turns her focus back on the road as they continue to drive in silence.

*****

"Are you hungry? I'm about to pull over and get some lunch. It's about that time," Reggie says.

Heavenly replies, "No thank you. I will just stay in the car. I ate breakfast not too long ago." Heavenly's mind still cannot wrap around his new attitude. Reggie doesn't want to be seen with her. Is he embarrassed by her? Maybe he doesn't like her the way she likes him, or is it because she is younger than him? Either way, she believes once she reveals what is on her mind, he will definitely change the way he treats her. She is still going to move forward with her plans to lose her virginity to Reggie. Heavenly watches Reggie closely as he walks to the car. She loves the fact that he is so handsome and tall.

"Before we leave, are you sure you don't want anything to eat?" Reggie asks.

Heavenly replies, "I'm not hungry. If I become hungry, I will let you know."

Reggie replies, "Cool, then we are headed to the hotel room." He pulls out of the parking lot to go back to the hotel.

*****

Christine and Theresa pull up to her house. They both hesitate to get out of the car, not knowing what they will walk into. Christine uses her key to unlock the door. As she turns the knob, a sudden nervousness overcomes her and she dreads going into the house. She looks back at Theresa who seems unbothered and says, "Help me get some of the children's things as I go get some of my things."

219

Theresa nods her head in agreement with Christine as she opens the door. They both take a step back as the odor hits them. Christine runs to the side of the porch to vomit and Theresa assists her by holding her hair back as she says, "This house has to be aired out. I see he leaves his mark everywhere he goes, even in heaven or hell, wherever he may reside."

Christine responds through her episode of vomiting. "I can't go in there. My stomach can't take it. Can you get our things, please? I will wait for you. I don't care what you grab."

Theresa replies, "I will go in, but this shit look a mess and it stinks in there, so you are right. I will be grabbing anything." Theresa walks in the house with a napkin over her nose as she attempts to gather some clothing.

What Theresa doesn't know is that Christine still cares for Julian just a little bit as a human being, and to relive that scene would be too much for her. The smell gives Christine an excuse not to go in the house.

*****

Reggie is sitting at the table eating his lunch while Heavenly sits on the sofa watching TV. "Dang, the way you are eating, it better be really good," Heavenly says.

Reggie replies, "It sure is and when I am done, I'm going to take a nap too."

"I am not sleepy or hungry, but I do know hotel rooms are boring," Heavenly says.

Reggie chuckles. "Well, baby girl, most hotel rooms are for a quick, decent place to stay away from home, or a place where you get that quick…" He hesitates as he realizes who he is having a conversation with. "My bad, baby girl. That's too much for your virgin ears, so let's just make the best of it. When I wake up I will take you home. I need to make a run anyway so I can get the identification cards and social security cards. Do you have any idea of what you want your name to be?"

Heavenly responds, "I think I want my name to be Amber. Yeah, I feel like an Amber."

Reggie replies, "Cool. Amber it is."

*****

Theresa brings the bag to the door as she says to Christine, "I grabbed what I could. You are going to have to wash these clothes. They stink just like this house."

Christine replies, "Thank you so much. I will throw it in the washer when we get to your house." Christine locks the house back up and then she and Theresa walk with the bags to the car. They get in the car and head to Theresa's house to get ready for the children to come.

"Theresa, I feel a little regret for all of this. My children have no father and if they find out I was involved with his murder, they will hate me," Christine says with tears in her eyes.

Theresa responds, "First of all, Mark and Lindsey are still young. You can keep it from them. But Heavenly is the one you need to get under control. What do you regret? Getting revenge on a motherfucker who saw how he broke your heart and didn't even care? He messed with woman after woman, and also got Charlene pregnant on you. He left you and still wanted you to selfishly suffer by being there for him whenever he needed, but never when you needed him. So, if after all that you feel regret, you are a damn fool."

Christine holds her head because she knows what Julian had done, but now she is thinking twice about her actions because he is not here for her to be angry at anymore. "You are right, the damage is done and I must move forward." There is a sudden silence as they continue to drive to Theresa's house.

*****

Reggie awakens from his nap and he notices Heavenly is strangely staring at him when he opens his eyes. "Why were you staring at me while I was asleep? That's kind of weird."

Heavenly replies, "I just think you were looking kind of cute as you were sleeping. I didn't mean to freak you out. I was just admiring how handsome you are."

Reggie gets up, walks by Heavenly, and makes his way to the bathroom.

"Are you about to take me home?" Heavenly yells through the bathroom door.

Reggie replies, "Yes, I am taking you home. Can I use the bathroom and clean up before we leave? Damn."

Heavenly replies, "I'm sorry if it seems like I am rushing you. I was just asking so I can get ready." Heavenly walks away from the bathroom door, feeling rejected again. She does not know how to get Reggie's full attention, so she sits on the sofa and waits for Reggie to take her home.

Reggie turns on the faucet and places water upon his face. He cannot figure out what has gotten into Heavenly and why she has become clingy and seemingly obsessive. He exits the bathroom and prepares to take Heavenly home. "Turn the TV off. I won't be back for a while. Grab the keys and head to the car. I will be right behind you."

*****

"I see you have changed the decorations in this place. I really love the family room and the colors you have chosen," Christine says.

Theresa replies, "Thank you, sis, but go wash them damn clothes and your ass. While you around here talking about some decorations. The laundry room is down the hall to the right, past the kitchen, and you can find the towels and rags in the utility closet upstairs."

"I need you to get me some clothes, pajamas, or something please," Christine says.

"Go upstairs. The room to the left of the bathroom is my room. Go through the drawers and find something to wear."

Christine goes into the room and finds clothing to put on after her shower, then she goes to the bathroom.

*****

Heavenly and Reggie are driving through traffic. Reggie cannot wait to drop her off.

"I know I get on your nerves, but I don't have no one else. I guess I am putting too much pressure on you."

Reggie replies, "You good. Just learn to be more patient and you will get whatever you want. I know you don't know me well enough to know what I do not like, but you will learn eventually. So, it's really nothing to sweat right now. We need to be focused on you graduating and getting out of here."

Heavenly hears what Reggie has to say, but what she really hears is, "Be patient and you will have me all to yourself when we leave town," which makes her anticipate leaving before the scheduled time.

"You can pull over right here. I can walk home from here," Heavenly says.

"Are you sure?" Reggie asks.

"I am very sure. I need to think, so the walk would be good for me." Heavenly reaches over to give Reggie a hug and she kisses him on his cheek.

He says, "Make sure you call or text me tonight. We need to start putting things into play."

Heavenly replies, "I will call you later," as she gets out of the car and begins to walk to home.

Reggie hopes he has not been too harsh to Heavenly because he needs her to continue to want him so his plan can go in perfect order.

*****

Theresa pours her glass of Cognac as she sits in the kitchen waiting for Christine to get out of the shower. Christine gets dressed and heads downstairs to talk with Theresa and make some dinner for the children.

"I want to make dinner for the children. What do you have that is quick but filling?" Christine asks.

Theresa replies, "I don't know. Look in there and find something."

Christine looks through the cabinet and freezer and finds something to cook. "Baked chicken, homemade smashed potatoes, with stemmed Broccoli. How does that sound, Theresa?" she asks.

Theresa responds, "That sounds great, but we have to talk as you are preparing dinner. Plus no one is here, so we can get down to business. Can I ask you a question? And I need you to be honest with me." She looks at Christine with great concern as she says, "Are you done with the drugs? Because I need you focused on the outcome now."

Christine replies, "I am done with all that. I have been clean since I have been in jail and it feels great."

"Glad to hear you are through with that mess. I have your back on everything except those drugs," Theresa says.

*****

Heavenly walks up to the house and she notices Theresa's car in the driveway. She knows she is home earlier than expected, so she is going to try and sneak in the house, hoping Theresa is in her room. As she slowly turns the knob, it sounds like she hears two voices, but she can't really tell who it is. She closes the door. Two voices are having a conversation, and the one voice sounds familiar.

She tip-toes into the dining area so she won't be noticed and realizes that it is her mother's voice. She is devastated. How could they let her out? She committed a crime. Now she has to deal with both of them. She becomes overwhelmed as she sits at the dining room table to think things over. Should she go in there and act excited to see her mother, or should she sit tight and listen to their conversation?

*****

Theresa and Christine do not realize Heavenly is in the dining room as they continue their conversation. "So, what are you going to do about the life insurance?" Theresa asks.

Christine replies, "Well I have to go down there and get the death certificate and send it to the insurance company. It is going to take about thirty days for them to make a decision and issue the check, but in the meantime, I am cremating his ass anyways. Why spend all that money on a meaningless funeral?"

"You're his wife," Theresa says, "so that would be your choice, but how will you get the money to Slim that you owe him?"

"I will use Angie Ruiz again and open an account. I'll keep some money on his books and drop the other half to his mother as he asked me to."

"Slim killed Julian at your hire," Theresa replies. "Why would you use that name again so they can tie you to the crime? Pay a random chick that needs a few dollars. Have her drop that on the books and I will have one of my guys drop the money to his mother as a kind gesture. You are asking to go back to jail your way."

"You are right. I just figured they never mentioned anything about that name, so I thought I could use it again. I am not going back to jail. I am finally free from love, stress, and financial problems," Christine says. She walks over and slaps Theresa up. They both smile in celebration.

Theresa looks down at her watch and says, "Enough of that talk. Heavenly will be home soon and we can't risk anyone else finding out. Too many people are involved now."

*****

Heavenly's chest starts hurting as her heart becomes heavy from what she just heard from her mother's and aunt's conversation. She knows she can't stay in the same house with the both of them. They killed her father, and it came out of their own mouths. She has to get leave and get in touch with Reggie. Plans have changed and she wants to leave now. She runs out the door and far away from these natural born killers.

*****

"Did you hear that? Sounds like the door," Christine says.

"It's probably Heavenly." Theresa calls out Heavenly's name. "Heavenly, I am in here." There is no response to Theresa's calls, so she walks through the house toward the door and notices the door is open. She says, "You must not have closed the door all the way. Oh well, that little demon will be here soon."

She closes the door and heads back to the kitchen.

*****

"Reggie, we need to leave tonight. I found out what happened to my father. Please come get me," Heavenly says as she is fighting through her tears.

Reggie replies, "Wait, Heavenly, what's wrong? I can barely understand you. Where are you now?"

Heavenly takes a deep breath and says, "Please meet me at four corners. I need you right now."

"I am on my way. Stay there. I will get to you as fast as I can." Reggie makes a u-turn and heads toward four corners to pick up Heavenly. As he arrives at the location where Heavenly is, she runs up to the car in a hurry to get in.

She is crying profusely as she says, "They killed my dad, Reggie. It wasn't by accident. My mother and my aunt planned all this out. She is not even going to bury him. She's just waiting for the insurance money so she can pay Slim. We have to leave tonight. Please, I can't stay there with them."

Reggie grabs her hand and says to her, "I'm going to take you back to the hotel room. You will be safe there. I will set things up for us to leave tonight. I don't know if I can make that happen, but I will try my hardest to get us out of here tonight."

Reggie drops Heavenly off at the hotel and he leaves to get his plan started. He is thinking about how easy it will be to keep Heavenly and what she knows as leverage for him and his family to stay alive.

*****

Christine is in the kitchen finishing up dinner when she hears Theresa and her children. "Mommy, Mommy," screams Mark and Lindsey as they run up to Christine to hug her. They are all hugging tightly as they have missed each other.

Lindsey releases from the hug as she says, "Mom, are you home for good? Where is Heavenly?"

Christine replies, "Yes, baby. I will not be leaving you anytime soon. I haven't seen Heavenly yet. Do you know where she could be?"

Lindsey replies, "She is usually home before us and she don't have any friends. She just stayed after school."

Christine replies, "Well she will be here soon. I am going to finish dinner so you can eat soon. Go do your homework. And Mark, you do the same." Christine slightly worries about Heavenly not coming home, but it's not that late yet.

*****

"Heavenly," Reggie says as he attempts to awaken her from her sleep. "I have everything in place. When it gets dark, we will go to do identification and social security cards. We will go straight to the airport after that. Hopefully we can get a flight to wherever you would like to go. Where would you like to go?"

Heavenly sits up in the bed to take in all the information Reggie is telling her. "Reggie, I prayed hard to take all the pain away, but it didn't go away. I had a dream when I was asleep that I got married and I became a pastor. There is a school in Maryland for women who want to become a pastor. I want to go to the Bible Seminary."

Reggie replies, "I have a few connections in Maryland. We can go there. I will support you in anything you want to do. How will you go to college when you haven't even graduated yet?"

Heavenly replies, "I will obtain my GED as Amber and then go to college. I just want a new life and a new environment. Thank you so much for making it all happen for me." She leans over and hugs Reggie, but this time she doesn't want to let go. She lays her head on his shoulder for comfort.

"I am going to gather all my things and you can take my bag to the car. I will go check out. It will be dark shortly, so we can start making moves now."

*****

"Theresa, I am worried. It's about to be dark soon and Heavenly is not here. This is unusual for her."

Theresa replies, "I don't think you need to worry. She is a big girl. If she isn't here later then we can go looking for her and I will make some phone calls." She looks at Christine's worried face and walks over to console her sister.

*****

"How long will it take you to print this stuff out for us, Allen?" Reggie asks.

Allen replies, "It's almost done now, my friend. Just be patient. You seem to be in a rush."

Reggie replies, "I am kinda in a rush, but I do want it done the right way."

Allen grabs the IDs. "Here you go, my friend. You have a new social security number and new identification card. I gave you two with the same last name because you weren't specific about that detail."

Reggie replies, "That's just fine. She is going to love it." He thanks Allen and heads to the car where Heavenly awaits his return.

"I have all the important documents now—birth certificates, social security cards, and identification. Now we can go to the airport to get a flight to Maryland. He passes Heavenly the IDs and social security cards as he says, "Check this out, baby girl."

Heavenly takes one look and has a big smile on her face. "Are we supposed to be husband and wife, or sister and brother?"

Reggie replies, "Whatever you want us to be, that's what we are going to be."

Heavenly gladly replies, "I want to be husband and wife. That sounds good."

Reggie nods his head in agreement as they pull up in the parking area at the airport. As they enter the airport, Reggie instructs Heavenly to let him do all the talking. "Hello, can I have two tickets to Lanham, Maryland for me and my wife?" Reggie asks.

The clerk looks up the flights for that area and sees a flight that is leaving soon. "There is a flight leaving in forty minutes. I can book you on that flight. I would need your IDs and form of payment."

Reggie replies, "Here's our identification and also I will be paying in cash. You can give my wife the tickets. I will be going to the restroom."

"Ma'am, do you have any bags or carry on bags you need to check in?"

Heavenly replies, "No, we are leaving on a family emergency, so we didn't bring anything." The clerk passes Heavenly the tickets and she looks around for a place to sit while she waits for Reggie.

*****

"Hello, my beautiful queen. You miss me?" Reggie says as he talks on the phone in the restroom.

"Someone is going to be missing you, but it won't be me. Wait, there will be no one around to miss you," Theresa says as she chuckles.

Reggie replies, "If you touch anyone I care about, you won't find what you will be looking for."

Theresa replies, "Nothing is going to stop me, especially not your weak ass. What the fuck will I be looking for when I have everything I want and need?"

Reggie smiles as he says, "Heavenly."

He hangs up the phone, turns it off, and throws it in the garbage as he walks to the stall to urinate.

*****

Meanwhile, as Heavenly waits for Reggie, she notices the news is on:

Today, Christine Valone, the wife of Julian Valone the murder victim, was released on a $200,000 bail. The other *accomplices, Shawn and Andrew Smith, went to court for the arraignment, but both were denied bail. In addition to this case, Julian's mistress is in the hospital on life support. The baby is in good health and she is in guarded condition, and we hope they both pull through. They will be returning to court to start trial in 90 days.*

Heavenly gets up and walks closer to the television so she can hear that story again. She is devastated from the information she heard about the baby. No one knew about her being pregnant. A tear drops as she says out loud, "I will be returning to seek revenge for my father and the baby. I will see to it that all of them pay for what they did, especially my aunt and my mother."

www.ingramcontent.com/pod-product-compliance
Lightning Source LLC
Chambersburg PA
CBHW072225170626
46813CB00003B/1094